Romans 8: 28

And we know that in all things God works for the good for those who love him, who have been called according to his purpose.

**1** Stacey stood on the sidewalk, barely able to contain herself. Today was the big day. It seemed like just yesterday she was teaching and coaching at Harbor Middle School. Now, she and Jacob were opening their nonprofit for teens. Jacob would continue as director at the shelter while she would be director for their youth home. She looked forward to this for a number of reasons. As much as she loved their children, staying at home for the past three years had been more than she could bare. Had it not been for her mother-in-law, Rose, whose retirement came at just the right time to help her with their son, she would have gone mad. Juggling a new marriage, a new baby, her job, and Jacobson's outreach program at their church was overwhelming.

Their family grew quickly. Six months after giving birth to Joshua, Stacey was pregnant with their daughter. She was a *surprise* child—such a surprise that Stacey did not know she was pregnant until she was already five months. She associated the struggle with losing her last ten pounds and morning sickness to hormonal changes. Her best friend, Samantha, let her know about what happens to a woman's body after pregnancy, so she wrongly concluded that her body was just "out of whack." It was Jacobson who first suggested she could be pregnant.

*Babe. I think you're pregnant* he said as he held her hair away from her face. She hovered over their bathroom toilet. *That's not possible Jacobson!* She said between heaves. *Well, technically it is.* She swatted at him as she stood up to wash her face. *I think you need to take a pregnancy test just in case.* It was early October and volleyball season had just begun. Thankfully by this time, her mother-in-law had retired, and she or Jacobson picked Joshua up from daycare after school. Because of this, Stacy was able to get back to other things she enjoyed outside of their home. She loved volleyball and was also fortunate enough to have an assistant coach who stayed later with the players when she was unable to. It was hard in the beginning because she carried guilt from both ends. She felt guilt for not being able to stay late with the girls and guilt for coming home late to her family. It took a while, but she managed to juggle all of them. Having a supportive husband and family made it possible.

When the pregnancy test confirmed her husband's suspicion, and the doctor told her she would be due the following February, Stacey cried real tears. The agreement she'd made with Jacobson was if they had two small children at the same time, it would be financially better for her to stay at home. Yet she had anticipated they would wait until Joshua was in Pre-K before having another one.

As with life, it doesn't always goes as planned. After Rachel was born, the first few weeks at home were so bad that Rose opted to move in with them for a while. It could have been hormones, but Stacey was far more overwhelmed than she had ever been. In many ways, she felt she had lost her independence and identity. Jacobson was as caring and doting a father as he was husband but having to adjust to depend on him financially was challenging. She felt as if her soul broke each time she had to ask him for something. It took having a come-to-Jesus meeting for him to realize what the real issue was and after months of reassurance, she was finally comfortable enough to rid herself of the burden of thinking she was making his life harder than it was. She realized she was being completely irrational and unfair to him because there was nothing he took greater pride in than taking care of his wife and children.

Even then, Stacey did not just give all her time to her family. She still very much wanted to be involved in her community, so Rose kept the children twice a week while Stacey volunteered at an afterschool program for teens. She was such a success with the kids that the director eventually hired her part time to assist with the program's activities. She started coaching volleyball and track, and the time outside of their home was a blessing for all of them. At first, Jacobson was concerned she would have a hard time juggling their son and daughter all day and then dealing with teens afterwards, but it brought her so much joy that he dared not interfere. Besides that, his mom was excited to spend time with her only grandchildren. It worked out for all of their good.

Now here they were. Standing outside their youth home for teen boys. She couldn't contain her excitement. Joshua had started Kindergarten and Rachel was at a childcare center not far from his school. Jacobson had begged Stacey for just one more, but she firmly reminded him they had one more sooner than she'd hoped for. She'd only been able to quiet him by saying that after their third child, Jacobson would need to get a vasectomy. At least for now, he had stopped mentioning it to her. It was still beautiful to see him with their children. Having grown up as the only child, it was the best experience she could ever imagine when she saw Joshua cuddle with Rachel for the first time. He repeatedly kissed her face as she smiled as if knowing that was her brother.

Stacey walked through the home and savored every moment. The home could hold up to twelve boys, ages 13-19 and they would get their first placement on tomorrow. A sixteen-year-old boy who had apparently spent the last year in a juvenile detention center. She hadn't received much more information from the social worker. She felt a mixture of excitement and nervousness. She was excited about what they were doing but nervous because she would be over an all-male facility. Jacobson, of course, would be a very present face and the "house parent" was an older gentleman, Mr. Lee, who had experience working with young males. With the support of their church and the community, she really believed the home would be an asset to and for the boys.

Stacey looked up and smiled. *Thank you, Lord, for all that you have done for me and my family. Please let us be a place of healing and safety for your sons.*

**2** Alexander looked around him in the cell that had been his home for the past year. After his mother was killed, he'd been in and out of the system for three years. Dealing with her death and being separated from his younger brothers caused a level of rage in him that he had been unable to deal with. Everything had been a fight. He fought at school. He fought his foster parent's children. He fought anyone who dared to correct him or interact with him. He was angry and there was nothing a counselor, teacher, guard, or officer of the court could do about it. Since he'd turned sixteen a few weeks ago, the courts decided to release him to a youth home instead of placing him with another foster parent. His case manager, Mrs. Brown, didn't believe that a boy his size, age, or background could be properly placed.

He had no idea where he was going and honestly didn't care. He'd go through the motions and make a run for it as soon as he could. *They won't look for me,* he reasoned. *I'm too old for them to be coming after. They'll just be glad not to have to deal with me.* The part of him that cared felt a twinge of sadness knowing that he didn't have a place but the part of him that had been hardened by life focused on a plan for his survival. He had no real skills but somehow managed to continue going to school. He had been able to get caught up in the detention center so he would be able to graduate in two years. Reality, however, would not allow him to be able to manage two more years of high school. He needed money, fast money, and the streets were the only way he could make that happen.

Mrs. Brown had other plans for him though. She managed to get him into some new teen home for boys and was working to secure a part time job at a local mom and pop store. Alex almost laughed when she told him that. *I can make more in one hour than they make the entire month* he reasoned. But he had to go along with it as part of his early release. His last crime didn't get him a slap on the hand like all the other times. He'd stolen his teacher's car and took it for a ride. His intentions were to steal the car, ride around, and bring it back before the day ended. He didn't even have a reason. He just didn't want to be at school, and she'd left her purse on her desk with the keys in full view.

Two hours later, the police found him sound asleep in the parking lot of an abandoned shopping mall. He was awakened by the sounds of sirens and voices yelling,

"Put your hands on the steering wheel and don't move!"

Everything at that moment moved in slow motion and all of his decisions up until that moment flashed through his mind. Alex had been in trouble at school, and even on the streets before, but they were always issues of fighting or trespassing. He'd dibbled and dabbled in drugs some and made money being a runner for Dee. Dee was more like a big brother to him. He never really wanted to get Alex caught up because he felt sorry for him, but he'd let him get in the game enough to be able to make some money on the side. There were a couple of times Alex had crashed at Dee's place after Dee saw him asleep outside near the park.

Dee's boys didn't really like Alex. They didn't trust him. They thought he was too soft and would end up snitching if something went down. Because of that, they stayed clear of him when he was around. Dee made sure they didn't bother Alex and that he only knew so much about what they had going on. It wasn't until one of Dee's boys, Russ, cornered Alex that they realized Alex had a soldier's heart and apparently a lot of built-up rage. One fateful day, Russ decided it was time to "scare" Alex off. Russ, Trip and Freddie thought it was too risky to have Alex hanging around. The plan was to rough him up a bit, but it went further than expected when Alex stood up to Russ. Russ initially had the best of Alex but somehow Alex pinned Russ and Russ's ego took it from there. Freddie and Trip tried to break it up, but Dee held them back. He was impressed that what he thought was a fourteen-year-old kid had the guts and strength to stand up for himself like that.

They went blow for blow even with Russ hovering over Alex by three inches. Alex was stocky and used his size to his advantage. The two of them were a bloody mess when it was over. The others in the room called a draw but Dee, Russ and Alex knew who the victor was. Russ didn't like him, but Alex gained his respect that day. Russ calmed down a lot sooner than Alex did. Alex held on to the anger much longer until Dee sat him down and talked to him.

*Young blood. You tryna die sooner than you need to.* Dee had taken Alex away from the others. Russ had called a truce as soon as it was over because all of them, at some point, had had some type of fight. Alex, however, was still holding on to a grudge.

*I ain't bother him tho' man. He came after me.* Alex reminded Dee of his brother who'd been shot two years earlier. He'd gotten caught up in the fast life which was why Dee didn't want Alex to get caught up. Now his brother couldn't even swallow food on his own. He sat propped up in a bed being cared for by their mom and a home caretaker. He had slowly regained use of his hands and was able to communicate with them, but it had taken nothing short of a miracle for him to make it out of the hospital. This was another reason Dee had distanced himself from his mom. He'd had so much guilt. He had not been the reason JT had started dealing but indirectly he had. JT idolized Dee and wanted to be just like him.

*If the streets don't kill you, all that stuff you got bottled up in you will. This ain't no way to live man. Some of us out here because we got to be out here. You got sense man. You got a whole lot mo' sense than most grown men. I'mma let you run for me for a little while longer but we gotta get you outta this. This ain't you.*

Alex knew that Dee was right. It wasn't him. He delivered once or twice a month and didn't spend money unless he had to. He didn't need to spend money on the latest clothes or shoes. Dee took care of most of that. He just wanted Alex to finish school and make it out of their neighborhood. After his mom was killed, Alex bounced around but was still able to hang out with his same crew. Eventually, however, he was sent to a foster family an hour away from them and they lost contact. Dee had mixed feelings about it. On one hand, he wanted to make sure he was alright, but on the other, he hoped he was in a better neighborhood with better people.

***

Before the incident with his teacher, Alex had been with his new foster family for three months before he ended up in Juvi. He actually liked the family. Mrs. Mattie was what he had imagined having a grandmother would be like. She was an older lady who had started to take him to church. She was so kind and loving that it started to break the hardness that had formed around his heart. Mr. Earl was a hard man, but his hardness was different than Alex's. Mr. Earl had lived through some rough times, so he was a strong man. He spent a lot of time working with Alex. It was uncomfortable for Alex at first since he'd never had any other men around him except his mother's drunken boyfriends, but Mr. Earl taught him to work with his hands. Alex felt a sense of pride when Mr. Earl would pat him on the back and tell him how great he was at building things. It made him want to be better, and for a brief moment, he was.

The day he had stolen his teacher's car had been particularly rough for him. Mrs. Mattie had been hospitalized with pneumonia and Mrs. Brown had come by to make sure that their home would still be fit for Alex to remain. She informed them that she would keep them posted in case Alex needed to be re-placed. Subconsciously, Alex would rather have been escorted out through his own doing than that of another. Even though he had no intention on taking a car that did not belong to him, something in him moved him to just go for it. He had already lost his mom and brothers so the thought of being uprooted from a place he finally saw as home just didn't work for him.

The day Alex went to court to face his consequences, he thought he would receive a fine and be sent to a new placement. Mrs. Mattie and Mr. Earl had been his fourth home in six months so he just figured they would send him to another home and place a monitoring bracelet on him. All the other placements had ended because of fights at school or with his foster siblings. Even when the others were the aggressors, he was the outsider and would have to pay the outsider's price.  He was wrong. On this day, the judge placed Alex in a juvenile detention center south of Dallas. He definitely did not see that coming since he had never really been outside of Dallas. It was the best and worst experience he'd ever had. It was good in that he'd been able to catch up on his credits but bad in that it had shown him how alone he really was.  After he lost his mom, his younger brothers ended up with their paternal family in North Carolina while Alex was left with nothing but a picture of them and memories.

Life was in no way easy for him. He was haunted while he was awake and even in his dreams. Every time he closed his eyes, he could hear his brothers screaming. *Don't let them take us. Don't let them do this Alex!* Alex closed his eyes as he laid across the bed in the Juvi. If he lived the life he had planned, he'd likely never see them again. They were seven and nine now. But if he stayed on the straight and narrow path, it would take him too long to get to where he needed to be. On either side of his options, there was loss and just like always, loss seemed to be his lot in life.

Dee had always tried to reach Alex. *Man, you think this life easy. This life ain't easy man. Always gotta watch yo' back. Can't trust nobody. Can't hear sirens without thinking they comin' for you. This life ain't easy. It's a fast way to nowhere.* Alex listened to Dee. Dee was the only one who had ever really looked out for him outside in the streets. Alex had never had his dad. Never even knew who he was. Rumor had it that his mama had been in a relationship with a minister at a church near downtown. They were engaged and everything. Ran into him at a tire shop across from her job waiting with what she later found out to be his wife and two daughters.

*Walked right past me like he'd never seen me a day in his life* she would ramble whenever she'd been drinking. *You look just like him though. I told him I was pregnant, and he swore up and down to Jesus and all the angels, he ain't slept with me. If I hadda been on the outside looking in, I would have believed him, but I was there. He was too. I thought 'bout tellin his wife but two wrongs don't make a right. Maybe that God he claims to serve can deal with him.*

At that time, Alex's mom wasn't on drugs. She would drink and party on the weekend but that was it. When her own mother passed, she dealt with it the best way she could. She ended up using and then ended up selling her body to get money for what she used. It was all a vicious cycle on repeat. He blamed God. He blamed his no count sperm donor, and he blamed the church for allowing a seed that tainted to grow from its soil. So when Mr. Earl came into his life and Alex saw a man who was genuine in his faith, it helped to erase some of the bitterness he had toward church leaders and men in authority. Every time he passed by a church, he wondered if his own father was seated in the front pretending to be someone he was not. He wondered if he even thought about the child he had left behind.

Tomorrow would be a day of new beginnings for him though. He needed to at least stay in place through the winter months. It was too cold to be in the streets. Besides, experience had taught him that people got real generous around the holiday season so maybe he could get enough money to get back to Dee. Dee could let him run for him until he figured out his next move.

Proverbs 16:9

We can make our plans, but the LORD determines our steps.

**3** Jacobson and Stacey waved goodbye to Joshua as they headed to the first day of their teen home. Stacey had barely gotten any rest. She had hoped the case manager would be able to at least give her some background of the boy they would be helping, but she had not. The only thing she told them was that he was sixteen and would be coming straight from the detention center. They didn't know if he would be permanently placed or if he would be released to a parent or guardian. Stacey hated being unprepared. Jacobson was much more relaxed about the situation because his experience at the shelter did not always allow for placements to come with files. Oftentimes, a mother and child would show up in the middle of the night and they would have to get the details of the situation later. Stacey had more of a teacher's mindset. She was used to her students coming in with some type of documentation. She was anxious so Jacobson took it upon himself to remind her what the word of God said. *Don't be anxious for anything but through prayer make your request known to God.*

"I know, Babe," she told him. "I'm just so excited. It seems like it's too good to be true."

"But isn't that just how God does things?" Jacobson asked. "Look how quickly our lives have gone. It's like we were launched into our destiny." They reminisced on all the things that led to their meeting. "It seemed like until we met, everything in my life went in slow motion."

Stacey put her hand on his shoulder as they headed down the highway.

"I feel the same way. It's so hard to believe this is my life. I'm so thankful. Every day I look at you and our children and I thank God for His hand upon my life. Our lives."

Jacobson grabbed Stacey's hand and kissed it. Their six-year anniversary was coming up, and he had a special surprise for her. Since Stacey had gotten pregnant with Joshua on their honeymoon and was pregnant with Rachel so soon afterward, their vacations had been weekend getaways to places they could drive. They had only gone on one vacation without the children. Now that Joshua was five and Rachel was four, Stacey was more agreeable to leaving them with their grandmother for longer periods of time. He looked forward to their anniversary and had a hard time not letting her in on the surprise.

He grabbed her hand and kissed it as they pulled into the parking lot of their newest most precious mission. The teens would be in a real home, not a center, and it had everything they would need to feel as if they were home. The large white wooden home with the wrap around porch would welcome up to twelve boys at any given time. The boys would have to share a room and Mr. Lee would be there as the full-time house parent. Rose was also working as a volunteer. She was unwilling to be placed on payroll. Said she was enjoying her retirement but would happily help as much as she could. They all thought it was a great idea to have a grandmother figure in the boy's lives anyway. The timing was perfect for all of them. Rose had graciously stepped in for her grandchildren and now that they were both in school, she wanted to spend time in other areas. God had really blessed her, and she was in a good place in her life. She and Mr. Waller from their previous school had become quite an item. Jacobson, James, and Jackson were skeptical at first, but Mr. Waller was a decent man, and they all accepted that their mother deserved to have some happiness of her own.

"I'm shaking," Stacey looked at her hands and laughed.

"I noticed," Jacobson laughed. "It's okay. You'll be fine."

"Let's go, Mr. Perry," she said and jumped out of the car. Some things had not changed. Stacey was still very much the sprinter of the two and when her mind was on something, nothing else mattered.

Jacobson grabbed their boxes and walked toward the door. They had brought over a few items from their home to add to the new teen's room. For now, he would be the only one there, and they wanted to make sure he had things to do. Mr. Lee had already set up a basketball goal, and they had all come together to get a workout room for the boys. It wasn't much, but it was enough for them to have something to do since they could not leave the premises without adult supervision.

The program required for the boys to receive instruction on site for the first semester of their entrance. Rose and Stacey oversaw the boys' education so they found an excellent virtual schooling program that would allow the boys to remain onsite.

Stacey looked at her watch. The case worker and young man would be arriving any minute. Time had flown by quickly and the doorbell shocked them both.

"Oh my God!" Stacey jumped down off the ladder and quickly closed the curtains she had hung.

"They're here!" Stacey yelled and then froze. Jacobson laughed and pulled her toward the door.

"Alright, ma'am. Time to face the music."

Jacobson was the first one to the door. When he opened the door, Mrs. Mosley, one of the case workers assigned to the center, greeted him with a smile.

She pointed behind her to let them know their placement was coming.

"How are you Jacobson? Stacey?" They had spent enough time in preparation of the program to be on first name basis.

"Excited," Jacobson responded.

"Nervous," Stacey added.

The young man walked toward the door and for a moment, his hoodie covered most of his face. As he approached them, Stacey stepped backward.

"This is…" Mrs. Mosley began.

"Alexander?" Stacey whispered. Her eyes glared at the familiar face of her former student.

The teen looked up. For a moment, he hovered between embarrassment and joy.

Jacobson looked from the young man to Stacey, realizing that the young man must have been one of her students.

"Do you two know each other?" Mrs. Mosley questioned.

"Yes," Stacey stuttered, "he's my student from Harbor Middle School."

Stacey remembered Alex's chunky little legs running to her whenever he saw her. She remembered the day she stood in between him and a bully protecting him. Without hesitation and with no regard for protocol, she put her arms around him and held him. His arms stayed limp by his side as if he unsure what to do with them.

Mrs. Mosley stepped inside and nodded for Jacobson to follow her. She handed him the folder and went over Alex's situation.

"He officially has no one," she said. "He is a ward of the state."

She took a moment to discuss some of his background and handed him Alex's folder.

"You all are probably his last hope," she added. "We're running out of options for a boy his age and with his track record."

Jacobson finished up with Mrs. Mosley and looked through Alex's file. He wavered momentarily when he thought about Stacey having to find out that one of her own was in this situation. His heart melted when he read what happened to Alex's mom.

*I can't imagine having to live this boy's life,* he thought. No dad. Both brothers removed by the state. Mother murdered. No immediate family. No fictive kin. No one to even stand in to help this boy. *How do you live when you literally have no one?*

Jacobson thought about his own children. Although Stacey was an only child, she still had her father and close friends. He had his mother and brothers. He was sure that if anything happened to him or Stacey, that his children would not end up in the custody of the state.

*How is it possible to have no one?* For the first time, the realization of what they were doing hit him. At the shelter, the children came with their mothers and left with them. He had always had this image in his mind—that once the teens would leave, they would actually have someone to support them afterward. But at that moment, realization set in. He realized how important it was to make sure they connected with others so that the boys who did not have biological families still had the support of family.

He remembered Pastor Smith's sermon about family not always being blood. He said there was no race, color, or surnames in the kingdom of God, but it was only the Body of Christ. *We are all kin in different skin so let's treat each other that way.* Jacobson looked over at Stacey's animated conversation with Alex as he looked sheepishly around his new home. It all made sense now. God having Jacobson working at the shelter. Being over the community outreach program at their church. Opening the boy's home. Having workshops encouraging families to open their homes as foster parents.

"You never cease to amaze me," Jacobson looked up and whispered. "You are a good Father who does good things and will leave the ninety-nine in search of the one."

Jacobson placed the folder on his desk and walked over to Stacey and Alexander.

"I hate to interrupt this reunion," Jacobson started.

Stacey laughed and stepped aside.

Jacobson introduced himself and welcomed Alexander to their home. Alex was noticeably quiet but friendly. Jacobson knew that he was being cautious and rightfully so.

"Can I borrow him for a minute, Mrs. Perry?" Jacobson asked.

Stacey smiled and said:

"Just for a minute."

Jacobson showed Alex the home and walked him to his room. He wanted to get him settled. Mr. Lee would be in later as he had a family emergency that had taken him out of state. Mr. Waller and Rose would be with him for the night until Mr. Lee's flight arrived in the morning.

Jacobson studied Alex as he walked into his new room. He let him know that at some point, he may have a roommate, but for now, it was all his.

Alexander put his bags on the floor and sat on one of the beds.

"So, this is my bed?" He asked.

"If that's the one you want," Jacobson answered. "Or you can choose the one on the other side."

Each room had two twin sized beds, a computer and desk, separate drawers, and a sitting area. Jacobson looked around at how nicely Stacey and his mother had made the rooms. They had prepared three of the rooms early on but still had three more to go.

Jacobson watched as Alex's hands rubbed the comforter.

"I hope you like it," Jacobson added.

Alex looked around the room. He walked over to the computer desk and sat down. He studied the pictures on the wall, each one unique in its own way.

*I can do all things through Christ who strengthens me.*

*Believe in yourself a little more.*

*You were designed for purpose.*

"Am I allowed to use the computer?" He asked.

"Of course," Jacobson answered. "We do have some restrictions on the computer and there is a curfew, but you will need it for your assignments. We'll go over the do's and don'ts after we get you settled in."

Alex stood up and put his hands in his pockets.

"Thank you, Sir. Can I go back to Ms. Royce? I mean...Mrs. Perry."

Jacobson smiled.

"Yes. We are going to get you settled and fed and introduce you to some others who will be helping you as well."

**4** Alexander looked around his new room. Mr. Waller had come in to check on him right before he turned in for the night. He couldn't believe it.

*What is this about?* He wondered. There he was, surrounded by not one, not two but three familiar faces. He remembered Ms. Royce, well Mrs. Perry now and Mr. Waller had been helpful to him a few times as well. He knew the older Mrs. Perry too mainly from the accident. Before he had only seen her in passing. He was in middle school when he had last seen them, a chunky little boy naïve about life. Still believing that life played fair and gave everyone a chance.

Being there brought back all the memories he had tried desperately to shut out. He had been so used to his mom being the way she was that he never saw anything wrong with her. She had not always been that way though. His earlier years, she was the best mother anyone could ask for. For the first nine years of his life, it was just the two of them. His dad had not been in the picture, and he honestly didn't have much information on him. Only that he had left shortly after he found out about Alex, and his mother had never seen him again.

They lived in an apartment not far from his mother's job, but it was safe and comfortable. She was there to take him to school and there when he came home. Then one day, she introduced him to her friend. For some reason, Alex knew, even at a young age, that this *friend* was up to no good.

"Sup young blood? You packin?" The man laughed as he put his hand on Alex's shoulder.

"Stop playing, Larry. He's only nine and has no idea what you are talking about." His mom put her hands on Alex's face and knelt beside him.

"This is Larry. He'll be staying with us for a while. You can call him Uncle Larry, okay?"

Alex nodded his head slowly. His mother had never had a man around him and as far as he could remember, she hadn't been around anyone else but him.

"Till when?" Alex looked from his mom to Larry.

"Don't ask yo' mama nothing," Larry glared at him. "Stay in a child's place."

His mother elbowed Larry in the side.

"He is a child, and he knows his place."

Larry, seeming to take the hint of a mother's protection, laughed it off.

"Trish. You know I'm just teasing with him."

He looked at Alex and added,

"Just joking lil man."

For the first couple of years, it was nice having a man around the house. Larry worked long hours, though Alex couldn't really tell what he did for a living. One day, his mother came to him and told him he would be having a little brother or sister soon. He was overwhelmed with excitement. He had always wanted a sibling. It had been lonely having just his mother so having more people in the house and having a real family was exciting to him. Larry seemed to be a nice guy. He was very attentive and caring to Trish and made sure she and Alex had everything they needed. He was even nice to Alex or at least he bought him things. When his mother gave birth to his baby brother, Trish stopped working. Not long afterwards, she was pregnant again and gave birth to his second brother.

Larry continued to work, and his mother stayed home with their sons. It was during this time that he changed. Not only that, but his mom changed as well. Dealing with his mom was like dealing with two different people. One moment she was the mom who he had always known and the next moment she was saying and doing things that didn't make any sense. He remembered the times she would go into an empty room and start yelling for them to stop waking her up. He never knew who she was talking to or what she was talking about. Then there were times she would write letters to his teachers that made up entire scenarios that never happened. Like saying he needed to stay home for the week because he was exposed to chicken pox. He didn't even know what that meant. but he did remember staying home because his mom didn't get up early enough to walk him to the bus stop. Alex was young, but he had been exposed to enough things to know that something wasn't right with his mom's mind.

Larry was a different story. He started staying away from home more and more, saying he had to work longer hours to support their family. Time would prove that Larry had a lot more going for him than just long hours at the job.

Alex could remember waking up one night to the sound of glass shattering and his mother screaming.

"Get out! You filthy liar! I can't believe you!" He could hear banging on the wall. Alex jumped up in fear that his mother was being harmed. He ran outside to the living room and saw his mother's favorite vase shattered on the wall. His mother held his youngest brother in her arms as she tossed random objects at Larry. He remembered thinking that he needed to get his brother away from them which is what he did.

His first brother, Larry Jr. was still sound asleep in their mother's room, so he grabbed Jesse and put him in the bed next to him. He stood by the door to see if he would need to call the police to help his mom. Even though she had warned him never, under any circumstances, to contact the police because they would come in and take them from her. He did not understand that then but later, it would make sense. Everything would make sense.

Alex laid across his bed and tried to wipe the memories of that moment from his mind. He tried to stare at all the inspirational postings around his room and think about how he could get on his own two feet and get to his brothers, but the silence in the house made it impossible. He was overwhelmed by emotions that he had intentionally locked away.

Alex could hear Larry's voice growing more and more aggravated as his mother screamed at him about his betrayal.

"She's pregnant? You got another woman pregnant? She came to the house I *live* in with *my* children and told me everything!"

Trish could barely breathe as she walked back and forth through their living room cursing and throwing things at Larry.

Alex turned on the radio in their mother's room so his brothers could not hear her screams. When he was sure they would be fine, he snuck out of the room and peered into the hallway.

Larry stood there with his hands in his pockets looking like a caught man with no defense. He was so solemn that Alex would never guess what would happen next.

The last thing he remembered was Trish yelling that she was going to call the police and tell them how he really made his money. By the time she reached for the phone, Larry's entire demeanor changed.

"It looked like he was possessed," he remembered telling the social worker when they interviewed him.

"It's like it was him, but not really him."

Larry charged at Trish and grabbed the phone from her hands. The look on her face showed both fear and surprise at his aggression. Then he started shouting at her and saying that she had tricked him into being with her. He told her he hated her and everything she birthed.

The next moment was the moment that would change the course of all their lives. Trish reached up and slapped Larry across his face. Alex recalled the evilest laugh he had ever heard in his life. Larry started yelling at Trish saying she would pay for the moment she ever laid eyes on him.

Alex remembered hearing Larry walked down the hall towards the room he and his brothers were in. Trish, apparently realizing that her children were in harm's way, raced after him. Instinctively, she yelled out:

"Alex lock the door! Lock the door now!" Alex ran back into the room with his brothers and locked the door. He managed to push a trunk that held many of their clothes in it behind the door. As Larry pounded on the door, Alex grabbed the phone to call the police. Something in him told him not to listen to his mother's warning.

After that, things became a blur. The 911 operator was in one ear asking for the nature of his emergency and the sounds of his mother and Larry wrestling in the hallway filled the other. Alex remembered telling the operator their address and hearing his mother scream. His heart raced in his chest and then the screaming stopped. It was the loudest silence he had ever heard until it was interrupted by banging on the door. Alex looked from the caving door to the window and knew that he had to get them out of there.

He snatched the window open and just as Larry pushed the door in, Alex grabbed both of his brothers and jumped out of the window. As luck would have it, the neighborhood dealers were out on the street and saw Alex holding his brothers as Larry crawled out of the window behind them, knife in tow.

Seeing no other option, Alex ran straight to the dealers, and they, in turn, ran directly toward three little boys who clearly needed their help. One of the men ran in between Alex and Larry and pulled out his gun. Larry halted in his steps.

"Get them out of here!" the man yelled to his friends. The commotion had caused quite a few people to come outside so they knew the cops would be on their way soon.

One of the younger men in the group grabbed Jesse from Alex's arms and led them to a house across the street. Alex held Larry Jr. like his life depended on it and only the sounds of him whining made Alex release his grip on him.

"Stay right here," The man rang the doorbell, and when he heard movement in the house, he ran.

Sirens filled the air.

"Let's go! Let's go!" The men who had been Alex's saving grace fled as the older couple, startled and confused, led them into their home and locked the door.

It had been four years since that night. He had been numb when the case worker came in and told him his mother was gone. His life had gone from a high-speed chase to a slow painful crawl. He had had to identify the man who had killed his mother. He had had to stand next to a police officer and case worker to point him out in a line up. The funeral had been a blur as he had no immediate family. They ended up having a memorial for his mother in a small chapel next to the courthouse.

For the first few months, Alex, Larry Jr., and Jesse were placed together with an older foster couple. The search began to find family who was willing to take them in. Despite what Larry had done, his older brother and wife, stepped up to get custody of the nephews they had never met. From what Alex learned, Don was nothing like Larry and would be a great provider for his nephews. He and his wife had never been able to have children so there was room in their home and heart to care for them.

As for Alex, who turned thirteen right before the Davidson's were supposed to get custody of their biological nephews, there was no such option. They apologized to the caseworker profusely about not having the ability to care for an older boy and two small children.

“Good luck,” they added sheepishly as they picked up the smaller children.

The boys, now realizing what was happening, screamed for their older brother. They begged him not to let some strangers take them away.

*I couldn't help them. Just like I couldn't help mama.*

Alex rolled over and felt the first tear that had ever fallen since that painful night. His life, since being separated from his brothers, had been numb. He had never mourned the loss of his mother. He had never grieved. He had only one emotion that had driven him to run from one foster home to another—and that was guilt. He blamed the outcome of that night on himself. Had he called the police sooner, his mama would still be alive. He would still have his brothers with him. He even blamed himself for not telling his mother he didn't trust Larry early on.

Even when the police officers called him a hero for saving his brothers' lives, he could only think of the one he had not been able to save. His life seemed to be one never ending consequence of that one night. His case worker had arranged for him to have counseling, which he did, but after six months of sitting at a table doodling the same image of a broken heart, the counselor realized that Alex was simply not going to talk.

"He's completely shut down," she said. "But understandably so. He's just not ready to open up. He'll let us know when he's ready."

Alex removed the comforter from his bed and saw a Bible placed carefully underneath his pillow. He held it in his hands and noticed yellow sticky notes placed throughout. He opened up the pages to one of the sticky notes and read:

"I will not leave you as orphans; I will come to you." --John 14:18

Alex froze as he read the words over and over again. He had never gone to church as a young boy, but he had gone with Mr. Earl and Mrs. Mattie while he was with them. Yet he had never seen those words before.

*I will not leave you as orphans; I will come to you.*

He crawled underneath the covers with the Bible in his hands saying the same verse in his mind until he drifted off to sleep.

He fell into a deep sleep and dreamed that he was still a little boy. A man whose face he could not see walked up to him and grabbed his hand. In the dream, Alex was not afraid. He felt safe with this unknown man as they walked through places that would have been frightening had he been alone. But for some reason he knew he was safe.

**5** Jacobson walked into the room and saw Stacey kneeled at Rachel's bed praying for her. Every night, she and Jacob would pray at the bed of both of their children. Most of the time they did it together, but sometimes, one or the other would do it alone. He watched Rachel sound asleep between her teddy bears and dolls. Joshua had been the first one to fall asleep, and Jacob had tucked him in as Stacey gave Rachel her bath.

When she stood with tears in her eyes, he knew that her mind was on Alexander. If he was honest, both of their minds had been preoccupied with him. Jacobson had filled Stacey in on Alex's situation on their drive home. She had been silent the entire time, looking out the window occasionally wiping her eyes.

Knowing Alex personally had placed a different spin on things. They had always known they would be emotionally and spiritually connected to the young boys they helped but having a personal connection with them brought more challenges. Finding out Alex did not have anywhere to go was also another challenge, but the good news about the program was that the boys could stay until they turned nineteen and then transition to Young Living—the partnership developed with another organization to assist young men who had aged out of foster services but still needed support getting on their feet and established in their communities.

Jacobson could only pray that they would be able to help Alexander. His track record had shown that he had not been able to remain in the same place longer than a few months.

Jacobson walked over and kissed Rachel on her cheek. When he looked at Stacey, the tears in her eyes had been replaced with fire.

"We're not going to lose him," she said. "I'll fight anybody I have to before I let another person cause him harm."

Jacobson grabbed her and held her.

"And I'll be right next to you fighting every step of the way."

They walked out of Rachel's room so as not to wake her up as Stacey continued.

"I know God has allowed this for a reason." Stacey started as they headed towards the kitchen. Twice a week, Stacey cooked enough meals to last them through the week. It was also one of the traditions they had established early on—allowing them to spend time together.

Stacey started chopping up vegetables as Jacobson seasoned beef and chicken.

"I was praying for our family and our children, and my heart was breaking for Alex. I started praying for him, and it's like I could almost feel the heartbreak he feels."

Jacobson listened carefully as Stacey reflected on what she would call her God moments. Those moments that she knew that God was speaking to her.

"I was praying and telling God I couldn't imagine not having anyone, you know? I mean even when I wasn't speaking to my dad, I still had Samantha and her family. I had my students and the people at my school. Then, I had you." She added with a smile.

"I can never really say I had no one even when I felt like I had no one," Stacey grabbed the crock pot and filled it with broth. Tossing the vegetables and beef inside, she covered it and turned to face Jacobson, who by now, was rolling dumplings for the chicken. After far too many times getting it wrong, he could finally be trusted to do it on his own.

"But as I was telling God how Alex had no one. He was telling me that my thoughts were not true."

Jacobson looked directly at Stacey as she crossed her arms and looked upward.

"It's like He was saying, He never took His eyes off of Alex."

"Even when I read the reports of how his mother was killed and how he was able to get his brothers to safety, I can see God's hand."

Jacobson smiled as he placed the dumplings in the second pot with the chicken. It did his heart good to see Stacey gain her strength in God the way that she did. He watched her as she grabbed the laundry basket and headed towards the laundry room. He followed right behind.

"Even though those guys that night were up to no good, they still served a greater purpose. And who knows how that moment may have changed them. They had not gotten so heartless and hard that they turned a blind eye to three little boys who needed help."

"That's true, Stace." Jacobson added. He had never really given that much thought. Alex's file had included various interactions with the police and caseworkers so as to allow for a complete understanding of what he had gone through before his arrival. Alex had told the policemen that some men helped him. One had pulled a gun on Larry and the other had dropped them off at a house and ran when they heard the police sirens. They could all conclude what type of men these were, but on that night, they were godsends.

Jacobson recalled only a few short months before of a story about an eleven-year-old girl killed by two teenage boys. His heart had broken. When the news reported the teens had taken the girl, his initial thoughts were that they were not going to harm her.

*They're just trying to prove a point to the family. They'll see her as their little sister. She'll be fine.* He had been so sure of it. The night the news reported that the girl had been found murdered and that the boys were in custody floored him. Three young lives, not to mention the lives of their families, had been destroyed before they had even gotten started.

"The devil comes to steal, kill and destroy," Pastor Smith had said to remind Jacobson that we cannot allow ourselves to see people when we should be seeing spirits. "It's not them, Jacobson. It's the invisible that is leading them. As believers, we are guided by God's spirit, so we know when another spirit is trying to lure us out of God's path. But those who do not know Him cannot be led by Him, so they are open game. Anything goes."

Jacobson refocused when he heard the washer door close. Stacey grabbed the other clothes and they headed for the second round of their bonding time. Had anyone told him that he would enjoy cooking and folding clothes with his wife, he would have thought they were crazy. But the time they spent together was well worth every moment. They were able to accomplish their family chores and talk about whatever was on their hearts and minds. It was time that slowed them down enough to be able to check on their relationship and each other.

"And look at how this is all playing out," Stacey continued. "What's the likelihood he would reunite with not one, not two, but three people from the last school he'd actually ever finished." From what the caseworker had said, he had drifted through four schools in a short amount of time before being sent to the juvenile detention center. He'd been able to catch up on his credits through their credit recovery program. He was described as very mild tempered unless provoked, extremely smart and distrusting. He just didn't want to be bothered with anyone. No one could blame him for that though.

"I thought about that too, Stace." Jacobson added. "It lined up in only the way God could do it. We can only pray that he will let us help him."

Stacey placed the clothes in one of the baskets and looked up at the ceiling.

"Yes. We have to pray that God gives him the eyes to see that he's safe here."

Proverbs 4:7

Getting wisdom is the wisest thing you can do! And whatever else you do, develop good judgment.

**6** It was chilly for September. Texas seasons had changed drastically in the recent years. The temperatures had not only started to drop but the cold season stayed much longer. Alex sat in his room trying to figure out how he would be able to get back to Dee. He looked at the few items he owned and knew it wouldn't be a good move to try anything too soon. He had already talked himself out of leaving during the winter months but seeing Mrs. Royce and the others from Harbor Middle School caused an internal fight. On one hand, he knew he would be fine with them. His mind was clear enough to know they would help him, but his heart was the one that could not be trusted. He would be seventeen in a few short months and he was running out of time. Remembering Mrs. Mattie and Mr. Earl made it hard for him. He couldn't bear the thought of getting attached to someone else and then losing them. Right when he thought he had found a place to stay for a while, everything just went wrong. He wasn't going to wait for the social worker to pick him up on her terms. He was going to leave on his own. Thinking about the day he had stolen the car, something in him wanted to get caught. Getting caught was a lot easier than having to worry about if he would be removed from a place he saw as home.

There was a gentle knock on the door.

"You up, Alexander?" He heard an unfamiliar voice. He concluded it was Mr. Lee, the one who would be with him the most.

Alex looked down at the clothes he had slept in and ran his hand over his face.

"Yes, Sir." He stood to his feet and walked over to the door.

When he opened it, there stood an older man who looked like a black version of Santa Clause. Alex couldn't help but smile.

"I'm Mr. Lee," He reached out and grabbed Alex and held him. It was the same strength he had felt with Mr. Earl.

"Nice to meet you, Sir," Alex answered as he released himself from the uncomfortable grip.

"You sleep okay, Son?" Mr. Lee asked. Alex nodded his head yes and looked at the unmade bed.

"I'm going to make that up," He added.

"Go ahead and do that and get ready for breakfast." Mr. Lee smiled the smile that only a loving grandfather could have. "We need to get you a few things. Heard you didn't bring much with you."

Mr. Lee winked at him and walked away.

Alex fixed up his new room and went to the bathroom to wash up. He hoped they would get him a jacket or a coat. He had never been into name brand items. The only real name brand clothes and shoes he'd ever owned had been bought by Dee. He didn't care what kind of coat, as long as it could keep him warm in case he had to make a run for it.

The smell of bacon and butter filled the air. He walked in the direction of the kitchen and saw Mr. Lee fixing their plates.

"Have a seat, Son." He pointed at the table in the nearby dining room. "It's just me and you in this big old house."

Alex walked over to Mr. Lee and asked him if he needed any help.

"No," Mr. Lee held both plates in his hands and headed to the table. "Not yet. Next time though you'll be in here showing me if you can cook or not." He let out a hearty laugh.

Mr. Lee made one final trip to the kitchen to get juice and jelly for them.

Alex looked at the most beautiful breakfast he had seen in over a year. There was bacon, eggs, biscuits, hash browns and cheese grits. He'd never seen anybody put cheese on grits before, but it all looked so much better than what he'd had at the Juvi.

He hesitated. He had learned going from place to place to see what others did before he made a move.

"Let us bless our food," Mr. Lee bowed his head. Alex followed suit.

"Heavenly Father, we thank you for this meal that you have blessed us to have. We thank you for having a safe place to sleep and a roof over our heads. We thank you for the love you showed for us by sending your son Jesus to die in our place. Most of all, I thank you for trusting me enough to send Alex to me. Help me be to him what you have been to me."

Alex didn't know what to do so he just added an "Amen" after Mr. Lee finished his prayer.

*Help me be to him what you have been to me?* He didn't fully understand what that meant, but the smell of the food distracted him from trying to figure it out.

When they finished, he helped Mr. Lee clean the kitchen. It made him think about helping Mrs. Mattie after dinner. Mr. Earl would be propped up in the living room watching TV yelling at the screen while he and Mrs. Mattie would be doing household chores. He had enjoyed that more than he had ever admitted.

"You ready, Son?" Mr. Lee pointed them toward the front door.

Alex followed Mr. Lee outside. He opened the door to the van and they both entered.

"We need to get you a few things," Mr. Lee said while buckling his seat belt. "I don't know what stores you young'uns go to, but I guess we can head over to the outlet mall if that's fine with you?"

"Yes, Sir. That's fine." Alex answered.

"It's getting kind of chilly. We need to get you a jacket and a coat for when it gets even colder. You know this weather out here is as unpredictable as a woman's temper." Mr. Lee laughed at his own joke.

"Do you go to church? We don't force you, but we would love for you to come with us on Sundays. Just want to pick you up a couple of things if you do."

"I used to go and when I was in the Juvi they had people come out to us. It was optional, but I went whenever they came."

For some reason, Alex was embarrassed as soon as he said it. He wasn't really sure how much he could say without being judged. He already felt like a lost cause and didn't want to mess up anything before he had a plan.

"See things done changed a lot," Mr. Lee said as he maneuvered the van onto the busy highway.

"Back when I was in and out of Juvi, you didn't see nobody but the guards and the other kids. We didn't even half get to see our parents, not that I woulda seen mine anyway."

Alex stared at Mr. Lee. Mr. Lee looked like he was in his early sixties, a clean cut, jolly old man. Alex couldn't imagine him doing anything other than being a clean cut, jolly old man.

Mr. Lee looked at Alex and laugh.

"I know what you thinking," Mr. Lee, noticing that Alex had not put on his seatbelt, motioned for him to do so.

"You think you the only one been in trouble?" Mr. Lee said. "I don't think anybody been in as much trouble as a young boy than me. It took a whole lot of growing up and a whole lot of bruises before I finally got it together."

"What'd you do?" Alex instantly regretted asking. "I'm sorry. I had no right to ask you that." Immediately, he turned his attention and looked out the window at the other cars. He wondered about their lives. Where they were going and where they had been. He wondered if the families talked while they were in the car or if they just drifted off into their own worlds. He wondered if they were happy or if the children were being abused. So many questions ran through his mind looking from the outside in.

"Don't apologize," Mr. Lee reached over and gripped Alex's shoulder. "I tell my life story as part of my ministry. I want people to know what it looks like when God doesn't just save your soul but saves your life."

Mr. Lee's normally jolly face took a more serious look.

"Let me tell you a little about me now. You'll learn more along the way."

Alex sat up ready to listen. For some reason, seeing this old man who claimed to have had a troubled past gave him a twinge of hope.

7 "No, Mama, No!" Rachel screamed at the top of her lungs as Stacey attempted to braid her hair. She had never been really good at braiding, but Samantha had finally helped her to catch on. Sam, Jason, and the kids had moved back to Texas about a year after Rachel was born. The following year, Samantha gave birth to Elijah. They often had play dates with the kids but now that Stacey was back at work and Samantha was in nursing school, their play dates had dwindled. They did vow to meet up once a month with the kids and then every other month for themselves. Jason and Jacobson were on full time daddy duty during their girl time, but neither of them complained. The men had grown as close as brothers, so it all worked out for their families. Besides, Jason often said he needed Sam to get away sometimes, so she didn't kill him and the boys.

They had planned to go by the group home, but Mr. Lee had told them he would be out and about with Alex for most of the day. Jacobson agreed that they should allow them to bond since Mr. Lee was the primary caretaker of the boys. Stacey reluctantly agreed. Luckily, Jacobson was able to take her mind off of it by suggesting they all go bowling. Mrs. Perry would have all the children as she was the designated grandmother of Sam and Jason's children. Jason's mom lived in Ohio so they would visit her during the holidays. Ironically, his dad had died the same year Jacobson had lost his father. Sam's parents lived an hour away so last minute arrangements didn't always work for them.

The first time Mrs. Perry watched all four children, they came home early out of guilt to which she quickly chastised them all.

"If I had control of it, I would have a hundred grandchildren," she scolded them.

When they entered the home, they had expected to see total mayhem, but Mrs. Perry had the children in order like only an old school grandmother could. Caleb was the oldest and was sitting next to Joshua watching a movie and eating popcorn. Rachel was sound asleep in Jacobson's old room and Elijah was rolling around on a floor mat.

"Let them wear themselves out sometimes. You young people want to sit and rock and hold them. That's all good, but let these babies move around. They gotta get a feel of things on their own."

Jacobson laughed and gave his mother a kiss on the cheek.

"I don't know about a hundred mama unless James and Jackson plan on being fruitful and multiplying."

He ducked out of the way as she swatted at him.

"Well, the both of you can give me one more. That will give me six."

Sam opened her mouth to protest, but quickly closed it when Stacey gave her the side eye. Sam had had such a difficult pregnancy with Elijah that she swore tooth and nail she would never have another child.

"I think we can do that, Mama," Jacobson replied. This time it was Stacey's turn to give him the evil eye.

"Next time don't come back so soon," Mrs. Perry added. "I'll go get Rachel for you."

However, tonight, they planned to go to dinner and a movie, then burn their calories off at the bowling alley. There was a new movie grill they had been meaning to try. The reviews said the lounging chairs could rock you to sleep. The way they all felt, that could very well end up happening.

Getting them ready for their time with their grandmother set off an entire event. Rachel's screams could break glass. She always hated getting her hair done.

"Stop it!" Stacey spoke firmly letting her know enough was enough. "You are not going to big girl school next year if you can't stop crying every time we do your hair."

That stopped Rachel midscream. She had been so upset when Joshua got to go to kindergarten, and she had not. The only thing that calmed her was knowing she would be at his school the following year.

"Okay, Mama. It's okay." Rachel wiped her eyes. She was every bit of Jacobson with Stacey's stubbornness. From her skin color, to her eyes, to the way she rubbed her forehead when she was upset, she was his little girl. But that temper was something they had to get a handle on. Rachel had gotten into a couple of scuffles at her preschool, and they had been teaching her to tell the teacher instead of taking matters into her own hands. So far so good.

Joshua, on the other hand, was just like his Uncle James. He could have been his mini twin. He had James's same charisma and humor. He made friends easily and they were thankful for that. Stacey was thankful that the two of them were so close. Rachel adored her brother, and he was fiercely protective of his sister.

"Can I go to big girl school if I don't ever cry?" Rachel interrupted Stacey's wondering mind just as Jacobson entered the room.

"You can cry, baby," Jacobson came over bringing their overnight bag. "Mama just doesn't want you crying when nothing is wrong. But if something is wrong, you can cry. Okay?"

"Okay, Daddy," Rachel broke free from Stacey's grip and jumped into her daddy's arms.

"You like my hair, Daddy?" Rachel asked.

"I love your hair my Rachey boo," Jacobson answered.

Stacey shook her head and laugh.

"Well, I love your hair too Rachey boo," She mocked.

"Hater," Jacobson teased.

Moments later, they were all headed for Grandma Perry's house. Tonight, they would be staying since Mrs. Perry complained about them waking the kids up so late at night.

Sam and Jason met them at Mrs. Perry's house with kids in tow.

Just as they were walking off, Mrs. Perry yelled out.

"Now that you won't have any interruptions, maybe you can work on my other two!"

Stacey's face flushed, and Sam's mouth flew opened.

"Mama!" Jacobson could not hide his embarrassment.

"Don't act like I don't know how the ones in there got here," She added and walked back into the house.

Sam and Stacey busted out laughing.

"Maybe she's right," Jason said coyly. "I still want my little girl."

One look from Sam forced him to wave his hands in surrender.

"Okay, okay."

"Do you want me to have the boys sleep in bed with us from now on?" She asked.

"Oh, good grief, no!" Jason moaned. "I can't take another foot to the face while I'm sleeping."

They all laughed and headed for their cars.

**8** Alex placed all the items they had purchased from his shopping trip in his closet and drawers. Mr. Lee made sure that Alex had what he needed for the upcoming fall days. From what Alex had learned, he would be enrolled in a virtual academy with Mrs. Perry as his learning coach. He would be enrolled in a few days as a junior and had mixed emotions about it. Part of him coveted the thought of finishing high school, especially since he was so close. The other part of him felt like waiting that long was too risky for him. He dared not establish ties with anyone or anything because life was a gamble and somehow, he had always ended up losing.

Spending time with Mr. Lee, however, gave Alex a new way of looking at things. Mr. Lee had shared some of what he had experienced as a young boy. He too had grown up in the foster system because his mom had left him with his drug addicted father and never looked back. When Mr. Lee was in the 3rd grade, his dad had beaten him so severely that he had been removed by social services after a teacher reported his bruises. His father had beaten him because he had "stolen" food out of their refrigerator.

"I was hungry, and my daddy hadn't cooked so I got some food out of the fridge." Mr. Lee spoke quietly as if he had somehow managed to go back to that day.

"I remember I took some mustard and spread it on some bread and made a sandwich. Wasn't much else I knew to do."

Alex listened to Mr. Lee's voice and found no sorrow or anger. It was like he was telling someone else's story and not his own.

"Daddy came in the room, and I knew when I saw the look in his eyes, he was drunk. But this time, it was different.

Mr. Lee and Alex decided to grab something to eat and stop by a nearby park after they left the mall. The two of them found a place to sit and watched the young boys play basketball while the older ones served as coaches.

Mr. Lee took him back to that night:

"Ray. Boy, what you in here doing? Didn't I tell you to go to bed?" His father stumbled out of his room and headed towards him as he sat at the table quietly chewing his sandwich. At the time, he didn't think he had done anything wrong. He just didn't want to wake his daddy up.

"I was hungry, Daddy." He wiped his hands on a paper towel that had been left there since earlier. "I'm gone go in a minute."

Mr. Lee said he never even saw it coming. Without warning, his daddy snatched him from behind and threw him across the room.

"You back talking *and* stealing from me boy?"

Ray looked up innocently at his father.

"I ain't stealing daddy. I just made a sandwich." At the time, he had not known how much danger he was really in.

"You just made a sandwich? You always back talking. I ain't ask you what you made." His angry hand came down across his son's face.

He had been used to his father's aggression, so he thought that he would just toss him around a little like he usually did and then return to his room and pass out. This night, however, was different.

"It was like I was standing in front of the devil himself," Mr. Lee said to Alex.

"He changed right in front of my face. It was the first time I seen darkness. Like real spiritual darkness."

Alex listened intently as he chewed his food. He didn't want to miss anything. It took him back to how Larry had started to treat him when his mother was not around. Not the physical violence but the feeling that he should not be there.

Mr. Lee said after his daddy knocked the half-eaten mustard sandwich from his hand, he realized he had turned into a completely different man. As soon as he stood to his feet, his father's hand came down across his face again. This time, so hard, that he dropped to the floor.

"That's when I knew I was in trouble," Mr. Lee said. "Real trouble."

Mr. Lee said he debated on whether he should run, but he didn't have anywhere to go. He knew Miss Bessie had told him if he was ever in any trouble to come to her apartment. She had known that Ray didn't have anyone looking after him but his daddy and had offered to help. She was right across the way, but at that time, he was too intimidated by his father's presence to try to run.

When his daddy left the room, he wrongly thought it was over. Little did he know, it had just begun. Ray was heading to his bed, an old sofa in a corner in the den, but his daddy met him in the hallway. He had an old phone cord in his hand, but new fire in his eyes.

"Take off your clothes, Ray Boy," His daddy commanded. He froze. His daddy had never made him get undressed to get whooped before. It had never gotten that far. The most he'd ever done was slap him a couple of times or push him around. When he hesitated, his daddy's fury was fed.

"He started snatching my clothes off me. Part of me wanted to run. Part of me wanted to fight him. But I was eight years old." Mr. Lee was reflective. It was as if he had become the adult speaker for the child him.

"The first time that cord came down on me, it felt like hot fire had burned my body."

Mr. Lee went right back to the day his life forever changed.

He had curled himself up in a corner trying to keep the cord from hitting his face. He remembered the cord coming down over his flesh and could feel drops of blood rolling down his back. It seemed like his daddy beat him all night. He had hit him so many times that he no longer even felt it.

"I remember I woke up on the floor, and he had poured water on me. I guess he was trying to wash me off. But he was gone. I don't really remember much else about that moment. It's like one minute I was there and the next minute I was gone."

Alex had lost his appetite as Mr. Lee told the story. Larry had threatened to rough him up a few times, but his mama had never allowed it to get that far. It was hard for him to listen to Mr. Lee describe how savagely he had been beaten.

"What did you do?" Alex asked quietly.

"I didn't know no better. I washed up and got ready for school, "Mr. Lee responded. "Truth be told, Son. I was hungry. I went to school to get something to eat. Wasn't thinking they would see my bruises.

Ray had gotten on the bus with his little wrinkled shorts and shirt on. He should have known how that day would go when he looked into his bus driver's eyes. There was a mixture of horror and rage. After that, everything went by quickly. By the time he had entered the building, the principal had met him at the door with his homeroom teacher right behind her.

"Oh, Ray Lee," Mrs. Marshall said. Her eyes filled with tears as she looked over his arms and legs.

"Let's go into my office," Mrs. Smith spoked quietly. Her voice choked as she led little Ray to the principal's office.

"At that time, we didn't have counselors and nurses at our school. They took me to the hospital and started making calls from there."

The doctor who examined Ray said there were over forty lashes on his little body. He'd had to clean them and cover them to keep them from getting infected.

"In all my years, I have never seen a child this badly beaten," Dr. Morris spoke behind the curtains to Mrs. Smith and Mrs. Marshall. "My assistant has already contacted the police and social services."

When Ray heard they had called the police, he immediately started crying. He thought his daddy would be even madder if he got in trouble. His teacher immediately wrapped her arms around him, avoiding his bandages as much as possible.

"I think about that sometimes. I think that's the only time I ever felt real fear. Like a real fear." Mr. Lee pointed at his chest. "Something in me knew that I was never gone see my daddy again. No mama. No daddy. No nothing. Just eight-year-old me."

Ray spent the next few weeks with Mrs. Brown. Social Services allowed her to be his guardian until he could be placed. Since he had no next of kin, it looked very grim for him, but Miss Bessie, his neighbor from across the street, had found out about it and opened her home to him. His daddy had been arrested and evicted so they didn't foresee him causing any problems for Ray. The placement was supposed to be temporary, but as with life, it does not always go as planned.

"Was Miss Bessie good to you?" Alex questioned. He had been so engrossed in Mr. Lee's story that he did not feel the same caution he had felt in the beginning. He was eager to know what happened to him.

Mr. Lee took the remaining part of his cold burger and tossed it in the bag.

"She was good to me in the beginning," He looked toward the sky. "She was getting money for me to be there, and I think, at least in the beginning, she felt sorry for me. Her brother didn't though. He hated everything about me, and he made sure I knew it."

The sky had started getting darker, so Mr. Lee suggested they head for the van.

"You just gonna leave me hanging?" Alex asked. Surprised at his own boldness.

Mr. Lee laughed.

"Son. If we stayed here all night, you still wouldn't get all of it. We gonna have to pick this up tomorrow. I think that's enough for tonight."

For some reason, Alex knew that it was enough for Mr. Lee. Reliving that moment had brought on a fresh wave of pain. But Alex had so many questions.

"Can I at least ask you one question, Mr. Lee?" Alex stood and helped the older man to his feet. He grabbed the wrappers and tossed them all in the same bag.

"Just one," Mr. Lee smiled an encouraging smile.

"Do you forgive your daddy?" Alex needed to know that. Maybe later he would be able to ask more, but for tonight, he needed to know. Listening to Mr. Lee's story had opened a fresh wave of resentment and anger toward Larry. Larry had taken everything he had from him, and his heart raged as he pictured Mr. Lee's daddy beating his son the way that he did.

"I forgave him a long time ago," Mr. Lee nodded. "Had to forgive him. The heart can't handle unforgiveness. It can't handle that type of pain."

The two of them headed for the van and Alex replayed Mr. Lee's response in his mind. The drive home was quiet. He was glad it was growing dark because he had had to fight back tears—tears that threatened to mourn his own childhood and that of his new friend's.

**9** It had been three weeks since Alex arrived at the Youth Home. He was enrolled as a junior in an online high school with Mrs. Perry as his educational coach. Although the courses and teachers were 100% online, he still had to have an adult assigned to him as the responsible party to monitor his participation. They had set up a separate area for the boys to have class. Stacey did not think it was a good idea for any of the boys to be closed up in their rooms all day. She did not want them to feel like they only had "ownership" in their rooms, and she didn't want them to feel like they were in JDC.

It worked out nicely. Alex enjoyed the schooling and interaction with his online peers. He did not realize how much he needed and wanted positive interaction with others, and he particularly liked that so many of the others had enrolled in the online environment for reasons that were like his. He had learned that when his homeroom and English teacher, Mrs. Fitzgerald, had asked them why they were enrolled. He felt bad when he saw the number of students who had been bullied or mistreated at school. He had never really had that experience. All his problems were at home.

Mrs. Perry had also been truly kind to him. She was grandmotherly and teacherly all at once. She reminded him of Mrs. Mattie in a lot of ways. Her and Mr. Lee together were good for him. But he was still guarded. It was late November, and he still had to remind himself to stick to his plan. Getting attached to someone was not an option for him. The thought of getting attached to someone else and losing them was too much for him. He had lost every single person who had ever meant anything to him, and his heart warned him of the pain of losing yet another person.

"Your homeroom teacher called for your biweekly check in. She talked about how proud of you she was and how well you participate with the others in class." Mrs. Perry walked up to him as he completed his Geometry task.

Alex looked up and smiled, but his heart bled. The amount of attention they gave him was too much for him. It felt so odd to be surrounded by so many people cheering him on and he swore Mrs. Royce-Perry, as he called her to distinguish the difference, was his number one fan. She had brought her kids over to meet him, and little Rachel had started calling him "Big Brother Alex" to everyone's surprise. Joshua called him "Uncle Alex." It was funny to everyone but him. It was threatening and invasive. He could not have them growing attached to him. It was too painful and reminded him of having his brothers taken from him. But outside, he smiled. He smiled when Rachel and Joshua argued about who loved him the most. He smiled when they brought him pictures they had drawn of him. He smiled when they shared their candies with him, but inside, it hurt him deeply.

"Alex, as a part of our program, we have set you up for counseling. Mr. Lee will be taking you every other Tuesday at noon." Mrs. Royce-Perry had told him while they all sat for Sunday dinner. They had decided they would have dinner together as a house once a month. It gave them all time to settle down and enjoy each other's company. Alex both hated it and enjoyed it. Part of him wanted at least one other teen to come so it would take some of the attention off of him, but that had not happened yet.

Mrs. Perry had mentioned that it was God's way of allowing them all to focus on this one sheep. She had told him a Bible story about the good shepherd who had left all of his sheep because one of them had gotten lost and his heart longed to find the one who was lost. Alex did not know how to take that. He knew he was lost, and even though he was surrounded by people who obviously cared about him, he did not feel like he had been found.

"Mr. Lee?" Alex had waited until they all cleaned up and had gone home.

"Yes, Son." Mr. Lee sat back on the sofa and grabbed the Sunday paper he'd been trying to read all day.

"Can we talk?" Alex didn't even know what he wanted to talk about. He just felt like he was in the middle of something and nothing at the same time and needed someone to help him.

"Of course," Mr. Lee put the paper down and gave Alex his full attention.

Now that he had his attention, he did not know where to start. He had been having nightmares about the night his mother was killed and his brothers were taken. He would be trying to get to them, and he would see a man dressed in all black laughing at him as he ran toward them. When he would finally get to them and reach for them, the man would snatch them away and laugh at him. He would wake up panicked and ridden with guilt.

"I just," Alex looked away. He was overwhelmed with emotions. He could only hear the deep wailing that came from his mouth, and no matter how hard he tried to stop it, he could not. He had never mourned. When you are surviving, it is hard to mourn. Even at the juvenile center, he dared not show emotions. That would have put a target on him that he would have had to fight his way out of. Having them surround him and show him what he had always longed for had broken him. It had been almost a month and they were more excited about him as the days went by, and it overwhelmed him. Love is overwhelming. It breaks down walls that don't want to be broken.

Alex wailed into Mr. Lee's arms and even his embarrassment did not help him to calm down. For the first time, he realized that he had suffered. He had been able to see that his mother had suffered at the hands of Larry. He had been able to see that his brothers had suffered at the hands of the system. He had been able to see that Mr. Lee had suffered at the hands of his father, but he had never seen that he too, had suffered.

Mr. Lee's strong arms around him told him what he did not say. He understood what Alex had needed to say because he had been there himself. He knew this boy had real wounds, and real wounds took real time to heal. He felt a sense of relief to see Alex show what he had not been able to share.

The two of them sat on the sofa not saying a word. Mr. Lee finally released him and patted him on the shoulder.

"I know," was all he said.

"Thank you," was all Alex replied.

When Alex went to his room, Mr. Lee stayed up walking through the house praying. He prayed for Alex, crying out to God to heal his heart.

*You are the God who heals. You are the God who can take the pain of the worst things of our past. You are the God who can take something broken and mend it to be used by You. Help his heart Father. Help him to hear your voice and not be tormented by the memories of a painful past. Close the door to the enemy when he attempts to remind him of what he has done. Let him see Father that you work everything out for our good because you are good – a Good Father.*

Mr. Lee prayed through the night, not just for Alex but for the world. Alex was yet another casualty of war—spiritual war. He knew the power of spiritual darkness. This is why he had ultimately been able to forgive his own father. Growing closer to God through His Word, he realized the power of darkness. When he thought about his own father, Alex's stepdad, and just so much of what he saw on the news, he saw the enemy doing what he does best—steal, kill and destroy. He had not just killed Alex's mother, but he had destroyed a family and stolen their joy. Satan was a brilliant mind of darkness-a brilliant mind of darkness indeed.

He had to pray. It was his only weapon. It was the weapon of prayer and love that would heal Alex as it had healed him. Something in him told him that if he didn't fight for Alex in prayer, that the enemy would lure him out and take him out. He had read through his files that he had his visitation revoked at the Juvi because of a young man who had a record of drug dealing. Once the facility found this out, they had suspended his visitation. Sadly, this young man had been his only visitor outside of his caseworker and counselor. His gut told him to remember the name—Deion Malcolm—known as Dee in the streets. He'd also read that the young man's brother had been paralyzed in a drug deal gone wrong.

"What are you trying to tell me Lord?" Mr. Lee paced the floor as he felt an urgency in his spirit. Mr. Lee fell on his knees and began to pray for the young man, Dee, as well. Something told him that his interaction with Alex would either make or break him, and since he could not stop Alex from deciding, he would have to pray for any parties that would be involved. God doesn't play favorites because we do. He sees souls and Mr. Lee understood that to pray for their souls meant to pray for their lives.

A quiet voice in him urged him to be ready for a fight, a spiritual fight for Alex, because the enemy was determined to finish what he started.

**10** Alex sat on the edge of his bed overcome with emotions. He felt a mixture of relief and embarrassment after breaking down in front of Mr. Lee. The part of him that had held on to those old wounds was relieved, but the part of him that had to be tough was ashamed of what he perceived to be weakness. Larry had told him that crying was for little girls not boys, so he had learned to turn his emotions off even when he felt deep pain. Hearing what happened to Mr. Lee made Alex feel for him and himself. He felt the pain of two little boys put in situations neither of them had control.

"I just don't know what I'm doing anymore," Alex said to no one in particular. He was talking to himself in the hopes that God would somehow hear. He had to stick to the plan. The plan was to get through the holidays and get back to Dee. He couldn't take a chance and lose anyone else. He had already lost everyone he'd formed a relationship with, and his heart couldn't take another loss.

Thanksgiving was right around the corner, and time had shown that the days were in full sprint. He had already started to save money. He received weekly allowance for chores. Sometimes Mr. Lee would give him more when Alex helped him outside of his normal duties. He had a few clothes, shoes, and a heavy-duty coat. He didn't need much. He only needed to stay put for a short while longer. Maybe if he saved enough money, he wouldn't have to rely on Dee, but he needed to get to him just in case he wasn't able to secure a job.

For some reason, as he sat there, he thought about Mr. Earl telling him about a story in the Bible about Peter. Mr. Earl said that the pressure of standing with Jesus got too much for Peter, so he left and went fishing. Alex didn't really know what to make of what Mr. Earl was saying until he explained. *Peter went fishing because when Jesus called him, he was a fisherman. When he had failed at being who Jesus called him to be, he went back to what he knew – to what he was good at. He knew how to fish so he went back to fishing.* Mr. Earl placed his arm on Alex's shoulder and looked straight in the eyes. *Only you know what you were doing before God pulled you out. Don't be like Peter at that moment. Don't go back to the place that you were before he found you.*

Alex tried to reject what now seemed to be a warning. *I won't run for Dee. I'll just stay with him until I can get on my feet.* He didn't know God as well as Mr. Earl and Mr. Lee did, but he did know Him well enough to safely say He wouldn't want him dealing drugs. But he couldn't stay on the streets. The thought of staying on the streets was just not okay with Alex. He remembered all too well falling asleep on the park benches. It was far more than he could handle or ever wanted to handle again.

He looked around the room Mrs. Royce-Perry had spent so much time getting ready for him. She had even brought their middle school yearbook and placed it on his bookshelf. He had gone through it and laughed at his chubby face picture. It seemed like a lifetime ago. He felt like he had aged fifty years since then. The boy in the picture was happy. He was happy even if he wasn't supposed to be. His mom had started to behave very differently than normal but she was still his mom. Still the one who took care of him when he wasn't feeling well. The boy in the picture had family. Alex looked over at the mirror on his dresser. He still had the same baby face, but his eyes held great sadness. He looked into his own eyes, and for the first time, saw a broken young man.

His mind wrestled with his heart on what would happen if he stayed and what could happen if he left. He knew that the law would not come after him once he turned seventeen and that would occur in the Spring. He could leave and stay low with Dee until his birthday and then apply for jobs. He wasn't sure if someone would be willing to rent to him, but he figured Dee would be able to help him find someone who could put an apartment or room in his name. Dee was one of those guys that could figure out how to get anything even if it wasn’t necessarily the right way.

It was getting late so Alex decided to try and get some rest. He could only pray the darkness that chased him all the other nights would allow him to sleep on this night.

***

**11** The next morning he heard a knock on his door.

"Okay, sleepy head," Mrs. Perry called through the door. "Time for you to get up."

Alex rolled over and looked at the clock on the wall. It was 8:32. He couldn't believe he had slept this late. His usual was to toss and turn all night and just wait until it was safe to get up without waking up Mr. Lee.

"Just a minute, Mrs. Perry," Alex said after clearing his throat. He jumped up and grabbed a sweat suit and headed to the bathroom adjacent to his room.

"You must have been really tired last night. Glad you finally got some rest," She added before walking down the hallway.

Alex jumped into the shower and tried to remember if he had even dreamed last night. Normally, his dreams were the reason he had not been able to get any sleep. He remembered closing his eyes and waking up to Mrs. Perry's voice. His normal was to meet Mr. Lee in the kitchen as soon as he heard him. He threw on his clothes, ran a brush over his hair and tossed his other clothes into the hamper. He looked around knowing he would need to clean his area today because he took pride in having a neat place. It was one of the things his mother had shown him when he was at home. No matter what she was going through, she had always made sure her home was clean and her boys were taken care of. She had always been a mother to them. Had she not gotten hooked up with Larry, things would have been the same.

He walked down the hallway and went straight to his "classroom."

Mrs. Perry had already logged into her account to check for Alex's daily plan.

"Good Morning, Mrs. Perry," Alex went straight to his desk. "I'm sorry I'm late. I don't know how I slept that long."

Mrs. Perry walked over to him and gave him a hearty hug.

"Did you eat?" She eyed him and looked at her watch.

"Technically, you can't be *late* in the virtual world, and you still need to eat. Go on." She shooed him toward the kitchen.

Mr. Lee was not in his normal place. Alex's heart dropped. Had something happened to him while he slept. He walked around to the back of the house to see if he heard him moving around. He hurried back to the front with Mrs. Perry.

"Where's Mr. Lee?" Alex couldn't hide the fear in his voice.

"Oh, now. Don't you worry about him," Mrs. Perry walked toward him and escorted Alex back down the hallway to the kitchen.

"He had to meet up with Jacobson to get some supplies. They are working on the other rooms. The caseworker said there may be another young boy joining us in the next few weeks, so they're trying to make sure they have another space ready.

Alex grabbed a bowl for cereal and sat at the table. *Another boy?* That was exactly what he needed. He had started to feel bad knowing that he was going to leave Mr. Lee in the house by himself.

Mrs. Perry patted him on the shoulder.

"How do you feel about that?" She asked thoughtfully.

Without hesitation, Alex smiled a sincere smile.

"It would be great to have somebody else in the house."

"Somebody else or someone your age? What do you think the rest of us are?" She laughed.

"I'm sorry, Mrs. Perry. You all have been really good to me." Alex poured milk over his cereal.

"But yes. Somebody my age would be nice."

Mrs. Perry nodded at him. "I understand. I would feel the same way. You are surrounded by a bunch of adults and two little kids fighting for your attention."

Alex forced a smile. This was yet another issue that haunted him. Joshua and Rachel had grown extremely attached to him. He was worried what his exit would do to them. He had already been haunted by his brothers' screams. Having the thought that there would be two others added to his list of wounded just didn't set well with him.

"I can't think about that," Alex mumbled.

"Think about what?" Mrs. Perry asked. Alex did not realize he had spoken aloud, nor did he realize Mrs. Perry was still in the room.

"Oh," Alex shoved a spoonful of cereal in his mouth to buy some time.

"I was actually trying to figure out what to get Mr. Lee for Christmas." That was partially true. He did want to get him something. He also wanted to get Mrs. Perry something, but he did not want her to know that.

"That would be nice of you, Alex. I'm sure he would appreciate anything you gave him. Mr. Lee loves you. We all do." With that, she turned on her heels and walked back down to their classroom area.

Her final words spoiled his breakfast. He forced himself to finish his cereal, placed the bowl in the dishwasher and got ready to start his day. At that moment, he needed his schoolwork to distract him from all the other thoughts in his mind.

Alex finished his work for the day and offered to help Mrs. Perry with dinner. She was busy preparing meals and talking on the phone. Mrs. Perry had him clear his area and encouraged him to take a break for a couple of hours. Slowly, they had begun to relinquish his time to him. In the beginning, he was on a schedule like the one he had in Juvi but with a bit more freedom. The counselor stressed how important it was for them to transition him slowly from having all his decisions made for him to being able to make decisions for himself. When he was first encouraged to spend time on his own, he ended up just sitting on his bed waiting for them to tell him what he should do. Lately, he'd started back drawing which was something he picked up at Juvi. He had to admit he was pretty good. So good that Mr. Perry had bought him several art supplies.

He'd actually developed quite a skill for drawing blueprints of homes. Alex was fascinated by a new model of alternative homes. To his surprise, people were literally turning storage containers and concrete blocks into livable housing. Part of him dreamed about owning a home or homes. He would sketch out entire communities. It had become a new hobby of his.

A knock on the door interrupted him. Alex closed his sketch book, jumped up and walked over to see who it was. He opened it and was surprised to see a young boy glaring at him. Just then, Mrs. Royce-Perry hurried to the door.

"Hi, Alex!" I'm sorry. This is Mrs. Mosley's foster son. I think he got a little lost looking for the bathroom. He's playing with Joshua until we finish the paperwork in the other room." She winked at him and led him back down the hallway.

The house had been so quiet that he didn't even realize anyone other than Mrs. Perry was home. Alex sat back on the bed and stared off into space. He'd seen those eyes before. The little boy looked as if he was maybe five or six years old. Foster son?

Alex slipped his shoes back on and walked toward where he heard Joshua and the little boy playing. Joshua jumped up and ran directly to him once he saw him.

"Alex. This is Kaleb. He's my new friend." Kaleb held his head down when Alex looked at him. Alex could tell he was very shy, so he approached him carefully.

"Well, hello Kaleb. I'm Alex. Nice to meet you," he said softly. He extended his hand to Kaleb who looked down at his shoes.

"Thanks, Mister." He whispered.

Just then Rachel came running out of the other room with a juice box.

"Here Kaleb. Mama said you are probably thirdy." Rachel said in between gulps of juice.

Alex laughed under his breath. They had corrected her a hundred times that the word was thirsty and not thirdy, but so far it had not registered. She ran over to Alex and hugged him around his waist. "I missed you all day Big Brother Alex!" He knelt down and gave her a hug.

"I missed you all day too," he said in return. It hurt him to say that. It hurt even more that he actually meant it. "How was school?" Alex could depend on Rachel to occupy him whether he wanted to be occupied or not. Rachel told him all about her day at Pre-K and how her new best friend, Natalie, was out with the flu. She went on and on about how she missed her friend and had to play with her fake friends.

"What's a fake friend?" Alex asked. Curious of how a four-year-old would define it.

"Someone who's there but they won't be there for long." Rachel answered as she skipped back in the room with her mother.

Alex couldn't help but think that he too was officially a *fake friend*. By the time he turned around, Joshua and Kaleb were stretched out on the floor, fast asleep.

***

**12** The winter months had passed by quickly. The weather had hit Dallas much harder than the years before. The ice had shut down the city more than once, so it had been him and Mr. Lee for more days than had been planned. Mrs. Royce-Perry and the others had had to deal with the weather and Rachel being in the hospital with pneumonia. When that happened, Mrs. Perry had Joshua with her so she could get him to and from school. They had spent all of Thanksgiving and Christmas together and had even brought in the New Year together. He'd enjoyed the time he shared with them so much that for a moment, he changed his mind about leaving.

He'd also learned more about Mr. Lee's life. Alex couldn't imagine anyone enduring the amount of pain and abuse Mr. Lee had suffered who still turned out, from his perspective, a decent man. Mrs. Bessie had been a nightmare of her own and her brother was even worse to Mr. Lee than she had been.

"Ironically," Mr. Lee had told him. "I saw the man who abused me a couple of years ago."

Alex had sat upright on the sofa when Mr. Lee told him this. He imagined what he would do if he saw Larry face-to-face. He would kill him, and if he couldn't kill him, he would at least try. Mr. Lee hadn't done any of that. Instead, he said he felt sorry for him.

"He looked like he was one step from death," Mr. Lee said. "He couldn't have been more than ten years older than me but when I saw him, he looked like life had already served him his reward."

Alex couldn't believe what he was hearing. Mr. Lee had gone through so much and forgiven so much more. *Who was this man and how did he have the strength to forgive the way he did?* It made him want to forgive but only after he could serve Larry the amount of pain he had caused him.

Alex and Mr. Lee had grown very close. Alex felt like he was with family, real family. But he remembered the plan. His heart reminded him to make up his mind. His heart reminded him that temporary things must come to an end, and he needed to be ready to take care of himself. Working three days a week had helped him save his money. He learned the job quickly and worked so hard that his supervisor offered to give him additional days. However, the program limited Alex to a set number of days and hours per week. They did not want him so occupied with work that he failed out of his schooling.

Alex worked overtime at school. Luckily, after he'd proven success during his first semester, he'd had the restrictions removed from his coursework and could work right through if he chose to. Mrs. Perry admired his hard work but often had to encourage him to take his time. The information was fairly easy for Alex but more than anything, he at least wanted to finish his junior year before he left. Maybe he could find a way to finish in the future, since technically, all he needed was a computer. He'd learned that the school he was enrolled in was not restricted to certain students. It was an online public school he had never heard of. It seemed like a lot of the other schools catered to those who had resources and support.

His mom had never finished high school and he knew in his heart she would want that for him. She would want a lot of things for him. As long as he didn't get in too much trouble, he had a good chance of making that happen. Alex finished his last assignment for the semester and hit send. It was a bittersweet moment. He had managed to make all A's and only one B. He had two more days before he would make an exit. Everything was planned out. Sunday, instead of going to church with them, he would stay at home. He would pretend to be ill. He felt torn about lying to get out of church, but it was the only time that all of them would have plans. Any other day, someone would stay with him. He couldn't fake too big of an illness, or they would not leave him, so he settled on an upset stomach.

By now, they had left him home a few times alone to run errands, so they didn't worry about him as much. Since he had been there almost ten months with no issues, even Mrs. Mosley felt that leaving him for a couple of hours at a time would be fine. The first two times he was alone, Mrs. Mosley was conveniently in the neighborhood and had stopped by with Kaleb. He wasn't as shy as he was when they first met. Just guarded. Alex wondered how long he had been in foster care and if he had parents to go back to. His questions were answered one day when Mrs. Mosley informed them that Kaleb's mother had met the requirements to get him back. Rachel cried like they had never heard her cry before. She had never had anyone leave her until then. Jacobson tried to console her, but she was inconsolable.

"Are you leaving too, Alex?" By now she had started calling him by his first name only. Her question took him by surprise. Luckily, her father picked her up and walked her away from the others. You could hear him speak quietly to her as her cries turn to occasional whimpers.

*I can't think about that. In a few months, she won't even remember me.* Alex convinced himself that neither Joshua nor Rachel would remember him. After all, they had had several boys come and go since then and they never even mentioned their names. *But you've been there the longest. They'll remember you.* His conscience told him.

Alex walked into his room and reached beneath his mattress. He'd stashed most of his money in an envelope. Mr. Lee had opened up an account for Alex because his job required direct deposit, so he had money in the bank and in his hand. Between money for his chores, gifts and his job, Alex had saved almost $2800. That would be enough to get him a room somewhere until he could get a job. He had developed a trust in his manager and had started dropping hints that he may need him for a reference in the future. He just made it seem like his time at the youth home was coming to an end, and he would be moving with a family member.

He started to rethink his plan to get to Dee, but Dee was the only one he had left. Alex knew that the streets weren't designed for anyone to make it on his own. He would need somebody just in case something jumped off. Dallas wasn't what people thought it was. It could get dangerous and once you were on somebody's radar, you had to move differently. When you were on your own, you had to move differently and when you were not known, you had to move differently. At least Dee was pretty well known. He had a few run-ins with the police and some locals, but he was mostly on good terms with the people in his area. His brother's tragedy really affected him in ways he never spoke about. It didn't stop him, but it definitely slowed him down.

Being around Mr. Lee and hearing what he had gone through until now had shown him other options. He could work with his hands and still survive. He picked up all the other envelops he had in place. There was a total of six notes. Two of them were cards that he had sketched for Joshua and Rachel. He promised Rachel that he would be back one day and not to be sad. He could only hope that she would not hold him to his promise but be comforted by the thought that he hadn't left forever. The hardest ones for him to write were to Mrs. Royce-Perry and Mr. Lee. He broke down twice writing to Mr. Lee. He assured him that he had been the best thing that could have ever happened to him and that he felt prepared to take it from there on out and asked him to pray for him always.

The next couple of days seem to go by in slow motion. He wanted them to pass quickly so he could make his exit and start his new life. Sunday morning came, and just like he planned, when Mr. Lee knocked on his door, Alex told him to come in without getting up from the bed.

"You okay, Son?" Mr. Lee's face filled with concern as he saw Alex balled up in his bed.

"I'm not feeling too hot. My stomach is a mess. I was in and out of the bathroom all night."

Mr. Lee hurried into the kitchen and came back with meds and warm tea.

"Here. Put this on your stomach. It should settle things. Was it something you ate?" Mr. Lee asked as he handed him a cup.

"I don't think so. It's been bothering me the past couple of days, but I thought it would pass," Alex lied. Unexpected guilt overwhelmed him.

"Two days? We probably need to get you to the Urgent Care." Mr. Lee stood up and beckoned for him to come.

"No! Wait!" Alex was not able to control the panic in his voice. "Mr. Lee. I'm sorry. You know I hate doctors. Let's see if these meds help first. Don't worry about me. I'll be fine until you get back."

Mr. Lee hesitated and wrote the number down to the church.

"I'm going to Sunday School and then I'll be back." Mr. Lee said. "I don't like the thought of you having a stomachache this long. It could be serious."

Mr. Lee closed the door and Alex waited until he could hear the footsteps go down to the other end of the hallway. He had not planned on Mr. Lee coming back so soon. Sunday School only lasted an hour. Luckily, he was packed, but he needed to look up an earlier bus schedule. Where he grew up was less than forty miles from the group home. The bus could turn that into an almost two-hour trip. He'd thought about calling a ride service but didn't want to start spending unnecessary money too soon. The sound of the van pulling out of the driveway sent a rush through Alex's body. He jumped up, grabbed everything he needed, and tip toed into the hallway. Just as he placed the envelopes on the counter, he heard the doorknob turn.

His heart stopped. There was no way Mr. Lee had been able to come back that fast. Then, he heard what sounded like male voices.

"We need to get in before the old man comes back," Alex knew immediately whoever was on the other side of the door was up to no good. Just when the men began to push up against the door, he heard a woman's voice yell out. It was Mrs. Royce-Perry. She had pulled up just in time to see the men at their door.

For a moment, Alex froze. His mind took him back to having to lock him and his brothers in their mother's bedroom, but a loud bump brought him back to the present. Mrs. Royce-Perry was screaming at the top of her lungs, and he could hear Rachel cry. Without thinking, Alex ran out of the front door and saw Mrs. Royce-Perry fighting for her life. He ran over and yelled at Rachel to get in the car and lock the door, but she was frozen in fear.

Alex looked around and grabbed the first thing he saw—a broken pipe. He charged the man who was on top of Mrs. Royce-Perry and managed to hit him hard enough for him to let her go. The man grabbed his head and rolled to the ground. By then, the second man had grabbed Rachel. Mrs. Royce-Perry let out a blood curdling scream and ran directly at him. She only stopped when she heard Alex yell her name. One of the guys had a gun.

For the first time, Alex saw the man's face. He put his hands in the air and said, "Hey man. Who you runnin'' for?"

The man with the gun flinched. He recognized street code. Whoever this young boy was knew the street code, and he didn't plan on that in this area.

"What you know 'bout that?" Alex looked down at the first guy on the ground and saw a familiar tattoo.

Alex held his hands up and made a sign. The man pushed Rachel away from him, and she ran directly to her mother's arms.

By now, the first man had stood to his feet, still holding his head.

He stared at him for a long time before recognizing him.

"Alex?" He spoke in amazement. He grabbed Alex and embraced him.

"Let's go." They ran towards an old car parked down the street.

Stacey had run into the house and was on the phone with 911. She made Rachel lock herself in the bathroom and told her not to come out until she came back to get her. By the time she ran back outside, Alex and the men were gone.

***

**13** The police were there for hours getting information. It appeared that there had been a series of break ins in that area. They had also initiated an endangered person's listing for Alex since legally he was a ward of the state.

Stacey replayed everything she remembered down to the sign and description of the tattoo. When the policeman suggested that Alex could have played a role in this, she shut him down. None of them believed that, especially Mr. Lee. Mrs. Perry had taken Joshua and Rachel into another room while the police went over the details over and over again.

"Is there anything else? Even the smallest detail will help us in this case," Officer Dan asked as they were closing out.

"Nothing that I can remember," Stacey sat as Jacobson squeezed her hand. "I just need you all to find Alex."

"We will do everything we can," Officer Reggie added. "Meanwhile, we are going to have a unit in the area in case they try to come back. I suggest you all be very careful the next few weeks. It appears to be random and a coincidence, but Alex could very well know these guys. You'd be amazed. Being loyal to the streets is more noble than being loyal to your family."

Jacobson walked the officers to the door. Stacey was far too shaken to stand to her feet. She had never been that traumatized in her life. Rachel finally came out of the kitchen and sat next to her.

"Thank you, Mommy, for trying to help me. Are they gonna find brother? He saved my life."

Stacey grabbed Rachel and hugged her closely. This did not seem real at all. It seemed like a horrible nightmare.

"Please God. I beg you. Please protect him. Please help us find him."

That night, everyone went home. Nothing they said or did could convince Mr. Lee to come home with them or go to a hotel. He assured them he would be fine, and that God had protected him all these years and would not stop now.

***

At home, Rachel wanted to sleep in the bed with Joshua. Normally, they would tell her to go to her own room but tonight was an exception. They knew she needed the additional support. Right before they tucked them in, Rachel prayed for Alex and the bad men. She asked God to tell the bad men to bring Alex back home. *Home.*

After they finished praying, Jacobson walked in to hear Stacey ending her call with Samantha. Sam had been checking in all day asking what she could do and getting updates. She had wanted to come over, but Stacey told her to give her some time to process everything that had happened.

Stacey stood in the kitchen looking out of the window. Jacobson walked up and put his arms around her. They were both quiet. She had hurt her shoulder in the struggle but had refused to get it checked out. She looked at her swollen wrist and the scrapes on her arms.

When Stacey had pulled up to the house, she only intended to check in on Alex. Mr. Lee called her on the way to the church to let her know Alex wasn't feeling well. Since Jacobson had to get to church earlier for the youth, he had already left home. Joshua was ready so he jumped in the car with his dad. Stacey hadn't noticed the men until she was already on the steps, and seeing them in dark colored hoodies, she panicked and scream. She knew Alex was inside and her daughter was with her. Her screams startled the one who had been attempting to push the door in and, instinctively, he jumped toward her. At that moment, Stacey only thought about Rachel and started swinging for dear life. The man seemed as if he was more so trying to get away from her than fight her back, but she was in full protection mode. That's when she felt his hands grab her and pick her up, but she managed to wrap her legs around him and when she fell, she pulled him down with her.

She remembered hearing the door swing open and seeing a flash run near her. It was Alex. She was trying her best not to let the man go because the thought of two of them after him just didn't work for her. She only knew that within seconds, the man went limp and rolled over on the ground. Blood seemed to shoot through the air like red lightning. By the time she jumped to her feet, Alex was heading straight for the second man who had somehow managed to grab Rachel and put her in between them. Stacey started to run straight at them until she heard Alex yell for her to stop. It wasn't until he yelled that she realized the man had a gun pointed directly at her child.

Jacobson listened quietly as Stacey recounted the story for him again. She needed to be able to tell it from a raw truth. With the policemen, she had been so determined to provide information that she hadn't had time to really process everything.

"He just ran at them with no regard for his own life," Stacey's voice broke. "I felt so helpless when he pulled that gun on my child. What kind of monster pulls a gun on a child?"

Jacobson rubbed her back to let her know he was there. He was struggling with so many emotions. Anger. Rage. Guilt. Shame. All the emotions that happen when a man cannot protect his family. He had only wished he were there, but had he been, it would have ended differently. He had already been in a similar situation early on in their relationship. The devil was busy, but once again, God had proven that He was with them.

"Stace. You did everything you could have done," Jacobson assured her. "It sounds like you were both protecting each other." His voice trailed off.

"Do you think?" Stacey started.

Jacobson knew what she wanted to know. "I don't think he had anything to do with it. Or at least, based on what you said, I don't think he did."

Stacey turned around and looked Jacobson right in the eyes.

"He knew them." Stacey spoke softly.

"Huh?" Jacobson could not hide his surprise. "How do you know? What aren't you saying?"

"The guy who he hit in the head hugged him once he realized it was him. My gut tells me he left with them just to get them away from me."

"Wait," Jacobson started. "What?"

Stacey recalled that after the guy with the gun let Rachel go, she had grabbed her and ran into the house. She ran to the phone to call 911 and locked Rachel in a room. She was just about to run back outside when she swung the door open and saw the other guy embrace Alex. That's when they took off running, and she stood in the doorway screaming for him to come back.

"Stacey!" Jacobson's voice rose. "Why didn't you tell the police everything?"

He took a step back in order to put distance in between them. He was going to force her to look at him and tell him what else she knew.

"Because I knew they would think he had something to do with it."

Jacobson fought to control his anger. Here he was thinking that Alex was a victim and now he thought differently.

Stacey could read his mind.

"Jacobson. Please," She reached for him. For the first time since they had been married, he pushed her arm away and walked out of the room.

Stacey stood in disbelief. She understood his anger. Anxiety swelled in her chest, and she fought hard to control her breathing. She grabbed her inhaler and quietly walked outside.

***

**14** Jacobson fought to control his emotions. He hated when he allowed anger to overtake him because it was hard for him to control it once it happened. He tried to pray but couldn't. All he kept seeing was opening a home for these young men to help them and having his family's life put in danger for doing so. His mind was all over the place. He was going to have to find someone to replace Stacey. There was no way he was going to put her in that situation again. He wouldn't even allow her or his children to visit. He was also going to replace his mom. He would need an all-male staff, and he needed them armed. His thoughts were everywhere. The more he thought, the angrier he became.

To think that he had even put Mr. Lee's life in danger after everything he had been through with Alex. They had brought him into their lives and look what they had gotten in return. First thing in the morning, he was going to the police department and telling them what Stacey had not.

***

Stacey sat outside on Rachel's swing rocking back and forth. The only light she could see was the one from their bedroom window. She knew exactly what Jacobson was thinking. She also knew it was pointless to talk to him once he was in that mode. Now that the adrenaline had past, every part of her body was sore. Her wrist was swollen, and her jaw was beginning to become stiff. It must have been from the fall. When she'd landed, the man landed on top of her, and his chest crashed right into her face.

*Father, thank you for protection. I know you were there. Had you not been there, this would have gone so differently. I know you did not send Alex to us to bring us harm. I know you sent him to us as a place of safety. The enemy comes to steal, kill, and destroy. But you sent your son for us to have life and have it more abundantly. Please protect Alex. Please help him to make the necessary decisions to get away from them. Heal the part of him that doesn't think he deserves to be loved and please. Do what you need to do to get those men away from him once and for all. One more thing. Can you talk to your son, my husband please? Let him know that Alex didn't plan this. Please let us both know that he had nothing to do with this.*

***

Mr. Lee had spent most of the night walking through their home praying for Alex. It was hours later that he found the envelopes on the counter with Alex's writing on each one of them. His heart pounded in his chest.

"What have you done, Alex?" Mr. Lee wondered out loud. He grabbed the envelopes and headed straight for Alex's room. The police had looked through the home but since they had not gotten in, they didn't feel the need to go through everything. Plus, Stacey had assured them that Alex had nothing to do with it and that their focus should be on finding him and getting him back home. Yet Mr. Lee decided to turn on the lights and take a good look through their home. Something just didn't add up about everything that had happened. He found Alex's suitcase fully packed and an envelop filled with money.

"So, you *were* leaving?" Mr. Lee sat on the edge of Alex's bed. He sifted through the letters and opened the one addressed to him.

*Mr. Lee,*

*First of all, I want to say thank you. Right now, writing this is very hard for me. I've grown really close to you and I wish it could have gone differently for me but it can't. It has to be this way. I'm not supposed to really belong anywhere. I don't think God has that in his plans. So far, I haven't so I think it's best I accept that and move on. I will never forget you Mr. Lee and I hope that you never forget me. I hope that you always pray for me. I'll need it. Don't worry. I plan to work with my hands and with my head like you taught me. I don't want to be a statistic. I don't want my life to end up having meant nothing in this world. One day I hope to matter to someone the way you matter to me. I wish I could say bye but I can't. I'll just say thank you and I pray that you can somehow forgive me for leaving this way.*

*Alex.*

Mr. Lee stood to his feet and wiped his face. He spoke out loud with passion and fury.

"Oh, no devil! No, you won't. You won't have him. You won't take him from our Father! He will live and not die and declare the works of our Lord. He will tell the world that you tried to take him, but God said no! No! No! No!"

***

The next morning, Mr. Lee jumped in the van and headed to Jacobson and Stacey's home. He needed to give them their letters and to talk to them about what he had planned. He wanted them to know so they could decide what to do with this new information.

He pulled up just as Jacobson was walking to his car. Jacobson had a look of determination on his face. He was heading to the police station and needed to get there soon. He was surprised to see Mr. Lee pull up.

"Mr. Lee," Jacobson walked over to the van just as Mr. Lee was stepping out of it. Jacobson could tell something was wrong.

"What's wrong?" He asked. "Did something happen?"

Mr. Lee looked around as if he were being watched. He held a newspaper in his hand and pointed for them to walk into the house.

"I'm sorry to come so early. I needed to get to you and Stacey," Mr. Lee spoke with conviction.

"Is Stacey up?" He asked.

Just then, Stacey came out of their room. She couldn't sleep and had been running on the treadmill when she heard voices in the living room. Whenever she was stressed, she would run. It reminded her of her track and coaching days.

Mr. Lee walked over and gave her a tight hug. She tensed up in pain, and he apologized.

It wasn't until the light hit that Jacobson saw the bruises all over her. He forgot about the anger from the previous night and walked over to her. He held her and gave her an unspoken apology. Stacey smiled to let him know it was okay.

Mr. Lee sat down and told them what he found. He gave them their letters. The room was eerily quiet.

Jacobson spoke first.

"He knew the guys. We discussed that last night." Stacey's hands shook as she held the handwritten letter from Alex.

"Now, we know he didn't have anything to do with it," Jacobson placed his hands over Stacey's. "You were right. We've got to figure out where he is and what to do."

Mr. Lee stood to his feet.

"I have a plan. His name is Deion Malcolm."

***

It felt like the longest week they had ever lived. Mr. Lee had not given them much to work with. He had everyone praying and made them all promise to give as little information as possible when the police contacted them. This new turn of events wouldn't work in Alex's favor. The system had already proven what it thought of young black males especially the ones who had troubling backgrounds. Mr. Lee had been very secretive. He only said he was going to get him back once and for all.

**15** Alex sat in the hotel room surrounded by the smell of cigars and marijuana. He had been with Russ and Jimmy since the day they had tried to break into the house. It definitely didn't go the way he planned. His plan was to get them away from Mrs. Royce-Perry and Rachel and to ditch them, but once they made it to Russ's car, he realized in the midst of everything, he must have left his money in his suitcase instead of placing it on him like he'd planned. He had his debit card but only had a couple of hundred dollars on it. He'd withdrawn most of it because he didn't want anyone tracking where he was.

Alex couldn't believe how things had turned out. Neither could Russ and Jimmy. The last time Alex had seen Russ was when they had fought at Dee's place. That had been years ago. Fortunately, time and Dee's words had helped him to forgive. Russ joked all the way to the hotel that Alex still had a mean left hook.

"Who was that lady?" Russ asked about Stacey. "Man. She almost took me out. I had to smash her to get her off me and she still didn't let go."

Alex had to hide his feelings. Now that he was out there, he had to make sure they stayed away. It looked like Russ and Jimmy had been behind quite a few burglaries in that area. The youth house just looked like an easy target because they usually only saw the old man and a teen kid, not knowing it was Alex.

Ironically, it had been Dee who had encouraged the truce between Alex and Russ. Now, Dee and Russ were no longer friends. Russ said Dee had gotten soft ever since JT got shot. Alex found out that JT died right before Christmas and Dee just hadn't been the same. He didn't want to run the streets. He was trying to stay on the straight and narrow. Alex didn't want them to know he was trying to get to Dee because it sounded like Russ had a lot of resentment toward him.

"Dee cost me a lot of money. Everybody know he was the lead man. We can't do too much cause them people he was working for don't trust nobody but him. We been 'round Dee all these years and still don't know who he was down for. Dee been locked up so many times, and the cops still ain't break him. So, when he told them he needed to step back, they didn't even stop him. All that money just gone down the drain." Russ passed a blunt to Alex who shook his head.

"Still lame, I see," Russ joked before giving it to Jimmy.

Jimmy was as slow as molasses. He had the IQ of a fish and was easily influenced. Russ convinced Jimmy that breaking in houses was easy money, so he went for it. Jimmy barely even got a cut of anything they stole or sold. But he did what Russ told him to do. It seemed like Russ was trying to be Dee, but in a different way. He didn't have the contacts to deal without Dee because the ones who knew him didn't all the way trust him. They used to tell Dee that Russ wasn't solid and would tell everything he knew if he had to. Alex believed them. Russ talked way too much to be trusted. Just being in the room with them for the past week already showed him that. He knew every house they had hit and every store they had robbed. But Alex started to grow weary when Russ found it funny that Jimmy pointed a gun at Rachel.

"Man," Russ laughed. "You need to stay off them pills. You gone shoot a lil girl?"

It took everything in Alex not to punch Russ right in his face. Russ read that part of Alex and told him to just stay calm. It was all in fun.

Alex felt trapped. Part of him wanted to go back to the youth home with Mr. Lee, but he knew Russ would come looking for him. For some reason, Russ had in his mind that destiny took him there. He would ask questions about what was in the house, and Alex would let him know there was nothing there of value.

"They don't even have a TV," Alex lied. "Religious people be tripping like that. You just gonna end up stealing a Bible."

Russ flinched.

"Naw. I still ain't read the one my grandma gave me before she died," His voice caught in his throat, and he jumped up to play it off.

"You hear that?" Russ asked.

"Hear what?" Jimmy asked while reaching for his gun.

"Fool," Russ waved his hand. "Stop grabbing that thing before you mess around and kill yo' fool self. Or worse. Me."

Going to what had been his home for the past ten months was not an option. Not as long as Russ and Jimmy were around. From what he had heard, Dee was not an option either. Dee had moved back in with his mom. Losing JT had taken a toll on her mental health, and he was working and taking care of her. When Russ commented that Dee would be better off dead, Alex thought it was best to stay away from him too. He needed to stay with Russ so he could watch his moves. Russ would have to kill him if he thought he was going to let him hurt Dee or Mr. Lee, so for now, he was stuck in a hotel room full of drugs with only the clothes on his back.

Jimmy walked over to Alex and handed him a pack of boxers and a T-shirt.

"Where you get that?" Russ asked. "Ah man. Never mind. You steal anything. I swear."

Alex was thankful. He walked into the bathroom and stepped out of his clothes. He only wished they didn't smell like smoke. Russ's car smelled like smoke, and the hotel room smelled like smoke. He jumped into the shower grateful he could at least change his undergarments. He took his few belongings and handwashed them with soap in the sink.

Russ called out to him while he was in the bathroom.

"Hey man! We gonna run up the street and grab some food. Be back in a minute."

Alex yelled out to let them know he heard them.

While they were gone, he sat on the cot that was his part of the room. He held his head down and for the first time since he'd been there. He prayed.

***

**16** Dee pulled up at his mom's house tired from loading crates all day. He had pulled a sixteen-hour shift and looked forward to coming home. It had only been six months since JT died. His mama was still struggling with that, but for the first time, he had seen a glimmer of hope. When he first moved back in, she fought him tooth and nail. All she could think about was the crew Dee ran with and the possibility they would come to her house.

"I've got too much to worry about Deion and getting my house turned into a crack house ain't one of them." She yelled.

"Mama. I'm not letting nothing happen to you in this house. Nobody's coming for me. I promise."

It had taken her a while to accept him. It took Dee apologizing for JT's death for her to realize he had always blamed himself for JT's choices.

"JT had a choice just like you had a choice. I taught both of y'all right from wrong. Y'all daddy. Bless his soul. Did what a man was 'sposed to do before he passed. You can't live your life guilty about what happened to your brother, cause just like you, he chose what he chose."

Dee was nowhere near healed, but he gained strength in seeing his mama come around. She had started going back to work at the Assistant Living Facility she'd been with for years. Her nursing skills were what had kept JT alive all those years.

"You think God still has a plan for me, Mama?" JT had asked her out of the blue one day. He'd finally been able to gain some degree of independence even in his wheelchair. He was able to move his arms and had limited movement in his legs. For a while, it looked like things were finally turning around.

"Of course, He does," Ms. Ida had told him. "God always has a plan. He can take everything that's wrong and use it for something right."

Every day for a week, JT asked his mama the same question. One day she asked him why he was asking her the same thing over and over.

"What's on your mind?" She asked as she helped him get into his bed.

JT sat quiet for a few minutes before he looked at her.

"I just think, for some reason, God has something for me to do, but I don't think it's gonna be here that I do it."

Ms. Ida stared at her son. Her heart pushed away what her mind was thinking.

"God can use us anywhere, anytime."

JT looked at his mama as if trying to tell her with his eyes what he would not say.

"It's okay, Mama. It's always gonna be okay."

"Yes, it is. Now get you some rest." Ms. Ida said just as she was standing to her feet.

"I love you, Mama." JT said. He'd always told her that, but this particular night, there was something forceful in how he'd said it. It was like he wanted her to remember it.

"Make sure Dee knows I love him too, and I want him to do everything I'm not gonna be able to do."

Ms. Ida spun around right before she got to the door.

She stared at him for a long time, fighting tears. *What is this child trying to tell me?*

"I love you too JT. You always gonna be Mama's baby."

She took one more look and walked out of the room fighting off the feeling of fear and dread. She looked at the clock. It was 9:00 p.m.

That night, Ms. Ida tossed and turned. She looked at the clock. It was 2:58 a.m. Finally, she got up to walk into JT's room to check on him. She felt an overwhelming sense of doom as she walked toward his room.

"I just knew," she had told her sister after she found him. "As soon as I touched his doorknob, I knew."

JT's death had shaken Dee to the core. He had always felt responsible for JT. Dee was five years older than JT, and their mama had depended on him to keep JT out of trouble.

Their family consisted of Mrs. Ida, her husband, Mr. Fred, Dee, and JT. They had been a tight family until Mr. Fred passed. Dee was a senior in high school when his dad had a heart attack at his job and died. He remembered it like it was yesterday. His mama had come to pick him up from school. Instantly, he knew something was wrong. At first, he thought something had happened to his grandmother since she had been sick, but when he walked to the car and saw her sitting in the passenger's seat, his stomach dropped.

They pulled off and headed to get JT at his school.

"What's wrong, Mama?" Dee asked. His heart pounded in his chest.

There was silence from the front of the car.

Finally, for what seemed like hours, his mama's voice broke the silence.

"Your daddy just passed."

Dee's mind began to spin. He saw his daddy laughing at him after he threw a fishing pole in and *caught* a log. He heard his voice reprimanding him when he caught him skipping school. He saw the way he kissed his mama after a long day at work. He felt his hands grab him when he spoke out of line to him or his mama.

JT's school was less than ten minutes from Dee's school. Dee never responded to his mama's words.

By the time they pulled up to JT's school, Ms. Ida had wiped her eyes yet again. When she stepped out of the car, Dee stepped out with her. His pain had no place now. His mama needed him. JT needed him. His daddy was depending on him to be the man now, and he would need to make sure they were okay.

***

Dee sat in the car in his mother's driveway. Lately, he had been thinking about all the things he could have done, should have done. He had started back having nightmares about JT. Even though his heart knew JT's death wasn't his fault, his mind would not allow him peace. There was a constant battle in him. Forgiveness is one heck of a thing. It's hard to forgive. But even more so, hard to forgive yourself.

Even his mind knew he had not been responsible for JT's death. His mind knew JT had chosen to drop out of school and to get caught up in the street life. Dee had dibbled and dabbled in everything trying to help his mama pay the bills. He'd lied to her and told her he was working at a warehouse, but he had actually been on the streets dealing.

Neither JT nor Ms. Ida knew about Dee's dealings until JT got shot. That's another reason Ms. Ida told Dee not to blame himself.

"That boy was already out there," She assured him. "He probably was out there before you got started."

"But Mama," Dee stood over JT's hospital bed wondering if he would even make it through the night."

"Don't but Mama me, Deion!" His mama was firm when she spoke. In her mind, there was nothing to discuss.

All of their lives changed that day. Ms. Ida, Deion, and JT. It was never the same for them nor would it ever be.

Dee sat in his car thinking about JT. Pain and laughter fought for their rightful place. He and JT were best friends. Even though they were five years apart, Dee had always been overly protective of his brother. Their entire family had been close.

"I just wish I knew you were alright, lil bro," Dee whispered to himself. "I wish I knew somehow everything was gonna be alright."

He painted on a smile and walked in to check on his Mama. The past week had seen a few good days for her. Being at work gave her a reason to keep going. She'd even started back fussing at him about how he kept his room. It was like music to his ears when she fussed. After months of silence, he could see her get her strength back.

***

**17** Mr. Lee sat in the living room waiting on an update from Stacey and Jacobson. He was not the best with computers and was depending on them to see if they could find out how he could contact Deion. So far, social media searches had come up empty. They had all thought that he would be able to be found on at least one social media site, but so far, what they thought had proven to be wrong.

But Stacey still had contact with quite a few people she knew from her Harbor Middle School days and sometimes desperate situations called for desperate actions. All he knew was that she and Jacobson were visiting an old-time friend of Stacey's named Mike. Mr. Lee could tell from Jacobson's reaction that he wasn't all the way pleased by her suggestion, but it looked as if Mike would be their best bet.

Mr. Lee walked around the home with Alex's letter in his back pocket. He had learned about spiritual warfare a long time ago. Not only was he praying for Alex, but he was praying for the two young men he left with. He knew what it was like to be lost. He knew what it was like to feel like wrong was the only option.

What many don't understand is that the system is not really designed to rehabilitate people. Even the smallest of charges could discourage an employer from hiring someone. Alex's offenses, as a minor, did not have to travel with him into his future.

Mr. Lee saw so much of himself in Alex. A young boy just trying to find his way in a directionless world. A young boy who wanted to do right but doing right took much longer time than he had to spare. The thing about being in a place of survival is that every day past that day seems too far away. Alex had a year left before he graduated from high school. Apart from the juvenile detention center, he had not been in any place longer than a few months. Mr. Lee understood and wished he had let Alex know that they wanted him to stay there as long as necessary to get on his feet. He wanted Alex to know even then, they would be there for him. He had not done that, and he wrestled with this in his mind.

But Mr. Lee also knew that words meant nothing to a heart that had not healed. He could have said everything right to Alex, and he would still have thought his stay to be temporary. Why would he think strangers would stay when the ones he had depended on so desperately had not?

"I have hope, Father," Mr. Lee prayed as he sat down on Alex's bed. "I have hope that you pulled him out to keep him out. I have hope that you brought him here because you knew you could trust us with him. I have hope that he will be back and that he will be okay."

His heart was determined, and his mind was clear. Once he heard from Stacey, he'd be able to carry out the rest of his plan. God had made Mr. Lee many promises and had never failed to honor them.

I have been young and now I am old,
Yet I have not seen the righteous forsaken

Or his descendants begging bread

Psalm 37:25

****

**18** Stacey and Jacobson pulled up to Mike's shop. She had not seen him since they parted ways. Jacobson was not overly thrilled about Stacey reaching out to Mike, but the circumstances needed an unconventional type of help. Mike was a changed man, but he still had access to the streets and knew them well. He had come a long way since his days in the streets, and his shop was doing so well that he'd had to open another one in South Dallas.

From what Stacey had heard, he was engaged to a wonderful young lady who had just recently passed her bar exam. It's amazing that time can put us in a place that we don't even recognize ourselves, let alone the people we once knew.

"Are you sure this is necessary?" Jacobson asked. Stacey unbuckled her seatbelt and hopped out of the car.

"Wait!" Jacobson called out.

"Hurry up!" Stacey yelled over her shoulder. "He's about to leave in a minute."

Traffic had been much heavier than they thought, and Mike had had to wait on them. He'd already informed Stacey he had an event that evening with his fiancée and needed to leave as soon as possible.

Jacobson rushed behind Stacey, finally able to catch up with her. He knew her well enough to know that when her mind was set on something, nothing else mattered.

Mike must have been watching because he met them outside.

Stacey reached out and hugged Mike and then pointed him to Jacobson.

"Nice to see you, Mike." Jacobson shook his hand and smiled.

"Nice to see you too, Jacobson," Mike's smile was genuine. Like he had met an old friend. Time and maturity had changed all of them.

"Let's go in my office where it's quiet." Mike led them to the back.

Mike gave them an update on what he knew about Alex. He knew the names of the guys were Russ and Jimmy and that the two had met only a few months ago. He found out that Russ was pretty much the leader because Jimmy couldn't really think for himself. He just did what he was told. Apparently, Mike had a couple of guys in the area on the lookout and said he would contact them as soon as he knew Alex's exact location.

"So, are these guys dangerous?" Jacobson asked. He wanted to know what they were getting into. There was no way he was going to allow Mr. Lee to go on his own or Stacey to go at all. "What am I looking at?"

Mike thought quietly to himself as if weighing his response.

"They're not dangerous because they're violent. They're dangerous because they're stupid. I think that young Russ has something to prove, but he's a coward. He'll get his boy to prove it for him. That's my only concern."

Mike wrote something on a piece of paper and handed it to Jacobson.

"I should know tonight where he is. I'll get that information to Stacey. But before you get there, text this number." Mike gave him the paper.

"Put in the numbers 611."

Stacey looked from Mike to Jacobson. She knew what that was for. Mike had someone on standby just in case it got ugly.

"I heard you fought one of them," Mike looked over at Stacey. "The one named Russ. "Heard you put a hit on the other one too."

"Yeah, well." Stacey frowned. Her face burning with embarrassment. "You know how that goes."

"Poor guy," Mike laughed. "I'm pretty sure he left with way more scars than you did."

Jacobson put his arm around Stacey.

"Yeah." He held her close. "I'm pretty sure you're right."

***

**19** By the time Russ and Jimmy came back to the hotel room, Alex was pretending to be asleep on the cot. His mind told him to interact as little as possible until he came up with a plan. He could tell Russ was the ringleader and Jimmy wasn't wrapped too tight. His finger was always on the trigger of his gun. If it weren't for that, Alex probably would have just fought his way out. He knew he could take Russ, and but for the gun, Jimmy too. He'd made up his mind to leave but had to figure out how to do it without sending off a flag to Russ.

Finding out Dee went straight was a relief for him. He already had to step carefully for the next few weeks until his birthday came so knowing that Dee was on the up-and-up was what he needed. He never had any intentions on staying out any longer than he needed to. Just long enough to get on his feet.

Russ had in his mind that fate had brought Alex to help them with everything they were doing, but Alex wasn't trying to get caught up again. The judge had made it perfectly clear that he did not want to see Alex's face ever again in his courtroom.

"You have a lot to live for young man and if you choose to throw it away, I'm going to make sure you don't take anybody with you," Judge Ingram said. "We are giving you another chance. What you do with this chance will determine the direction you go."

"Thank you, your Honor." Alex swallowed nervously. He still wasn't sure what was happening. Just a few hours earlier, his court appointed lawyer had contacted the detention center and informed them they needed to transport him to court that day. No warning. No preparation.

Usually, his attorney would meet with him and his case manager, but something had happened and apparently there had been no time to prepare.

In the few minutes before they walked into the courtroom, Attorney Ravenel, Alex's court appointed counsel briefed him.

"It looks like there was a request for you to be sent to a group home with a mentorship program."

Alex could not hide his confusion. He still had three more months on his sentence and was supposed to be transferred to a court appointed foster home. It had only been two days before when he received notification of his upcoming release date. So being abruptly removed from his room and escorted across the courtyard was unnerving.

Ms. Ravenel could feel Alex's nervousness and assured him this was absolutely a good thing.

"Someone bigger than us is looking out for you kid," Ms. Ravenel whispered.

"From the looks of it, they want you transitioned immediately," She smiled. "I'm feeling really good about this, Alexander."

Alex walked into the room and listened to the other cases before him. This was his first experience with this particular judge. Clearly, he was a no-nonsense judge who had likely heard every excuse under the sun and had very little mercy left to give.

"Don't ever think life is full of second chances," Judge Ingram warned him. "It very rarely is, and it looks like you have had more chances than most."

Alex couldn't tell if the judge was warning him because he didn't want him in anymore trouble or because he expected him to blow this opportunity. Neither one made him feel good about walking out of the detention center. Strangely, it had been the most stable environment he had been in in a long time.

He questioned himself for leaving Mr. Lee and the home. He'd been so focused on not getting attached that he had blocked out the judge's stern warning. His mind almost panicked thinking he could get in trouble again and be sent right back to Juvi. But it was all the more reason for him not to get caught.

Russ and Jimmy carried on as if Alex wasn't even in the room.

"I still think he lyin' bout what's in the old man house, man." Jimmy said as he shoved chips in his mouth and reached for the remote.

"I be looking at those group homes and you know folks give them a lot of stuff 'cause they feel sorry for 'em," Jimmy added.

Russ shot Jimmy a look that told him to shut up.

"I swear you act like the dude dead," Russ responded, annoyed. "He's sleep."

"So what?" Jimmy questioned.

Russ snatched the bag of chips from Jimmy and walked over to his side of the room.

"You really don't have no sense, huh?" Russ asked. "I used to think you was playing but you real stupid."

Jimmy clinched his fist and mumbled under his breath.

"What was that?" Russ asked.

"Don't call me stupid," Jimmy repeated. His voice had changed. There was an unfamiliar anger in it that Alex had not heard before.

Miraculously, Russ left it alone.

***

**20** Alex must have fallen asleep because he woke up the next morning being slapped in the face by Russ.

"Man," Russ laughed. "I swear I thought you was dead for a minute. We been trying to get you up for a minute."

Alex looked over to the bed and saw it covered with drugs.

"Aye, Russ," Alex sat up trying to get his mind clear. "You know that's a stupid move, right? Everybody know not to have stuff on them like that."

"I ain't worried too much, man," Russ started. "We bout to get rid of all of it anyway. Jimmy on his way out. You goin' with him."

Alex shook his head.

"Nah, man. I got court papers on me." Alex grabbed his shirt from underneath the cot and pulled it on.

Russ stared him down trying to intimidate him.

"I ain't ask you," he said forcefully. "I told you you was gone go with him."

Jimmy started putting everything inside his bag.

"I don't need him," he said. "I got it."

Russ walked over and grabbed the bag from Jimmy's hand.

"I ain't ask you either," he growled. "You ain't been thinking so don't start now."

To Alex's surprise, Jimmy grabbed the bag back from Russ.

"I'm sick of you acting like you my boss," Jimmy said. This time he stared Russ right in the face.

Just then, Alex spoke up. The last thing he needed was a fight to break out between the two of them. A room full of drugs and three young black males with records was bound not to end up in their favor.

"Jimmy man," Alex said while reaching for his shoes. "I'm going man. I'm tired of being stuck in this room anyway."

Jimmy and Russ were still face to face. Alex could tell Russ was just trying to intimidate him. Part of him wanted to punch Russ in the face and let the chips fall where they may, but something in him told him to wait. Patience was something he had always been forced to have whether he wanted to or not. A quiet voice told him it was just a matter of time before things turned. When that happened, he would be able to get away from them. Maybe he would be able to get Jimmy away too.

***

Alex and Jimmy stood outside waiting on Big Chris to pull up. His heart almost stopped when a police car started to trail them while they were walking down the sidewalk. It had been a long time since he had been out on the streets and time had changed him. His heart did not hold the same hardness, and he had stopped wishing that death would just come and take him away. It wasn't long before Big Chris pulled up. Alex remembered him back when he hung with Dee.

"Woahhh!" Chris jumped out of the car when he saw Alex. "Lil bro, where you been?" He reached out and grabbed Alex and pulled him in for a hug. "Man, I thought these streets had took you out."

Alex hugged Big Chris back before breathing a sigh of relief. It was good to know he was still the same Chris. Chris was a good guy with a bad past. He and Dee were best friends when Alex was taken into state custody.

"Good to see you, man," Alex said. He wanted to ask about Dee but wasn't sure they were still on good terms.

"You seen Dee?" Chris asked him.

"Nah, man." Alex started. "How 'bout you?"

"We kicked it a few months ago, but Dee been out the game since JT died."

Chris spoke briefly about the things that had happened to Dee. He told him how JT never recovered after being paralyzed. Apparently, things had taken a turn for the worse and this had gotten Dee's attention. Alex tried to hide his relief. It hurt him to know about JT, but it made him feel good that Dee had turned over a new leaf. It made him feel good that someone else understood his decision. To think. Just a few days ago, he planned to run for Dee until he got on his feet but knowing Dee wasn't out there gave him a reason to hope for something better.

"I'll let him know I saw you if I run into him," Big Chris said as he got back in his car. "He still gone be my boy no matter what. I respect anybody trying to do the right thing. I just ain't had no real reason to do nothing different. But who knows? Maybe one day."

Jimmy and Alex stood quietly on the sidewalk.

"I respect what Dee did," Jimmy said out of nowhere. "That's why Russ jealous. He wanna do something, but he don't know what else to do."

Alex was surprised to hear that coming from Jimmy. He didn't want to ask too many questions because he wasn't sure how much he could trust Jimmy. After all, he was pretty much Russ's puppet.

"What about you?" Alex asked.

"What about me?" Jimmy responded.

"You ever want to do something different?" Alex shoved his hands in his pockets and slowly started walking toward the hotel. It was cold and the hotel was a little more than two miles from where they were.

"All the time," Jimmy said. "But when my mama died, I stopped believing I could."

Alex could hear the sadness in Jimmy's voice.

"I know what you mean, man." Alex's voice was barely above a whisper. His heart still hurt when he thought about his mama and brothers.

The two walked back to the hotel without saying another word. Jimmy wasn't as dumb as Alex thought. He just needed help like everybody else.

***

**21** It was dark when Mr. Lee pulled up to the warehouse. He didn't really have a plan, but he felt God assure him he would know right when he needed to. Jacobson had already told him where Dee worked, but he had made Mr. Lee promise not to go without him. He still wasn't sure about Dee or what he was about. That morning, though, while Mr. Lee was praying, he knew he needed to find Dee. Something told him he needed to find Dee *and* Alex. There was an urgency that only came when God wanted him to move.

It had been almost two hours before Mr. Lee started to see people come out of the warehouse. He stepped out of his car and walked over to the first young man he saw.

"Son," Mr. Lee smiled. "Do you know a young man named Dee?"

The young man looked Mr. Lee up and down as if trying to determine if he was coming for good or bad. After a minute, he pointed at an older model car parked in the parking lot.

"He clockin' out soon, but his car right there."

Mr. Lee thanked the young man and waited close to the parked car.

Just then, Dee started walking toward his car. The life he had lived made him overly aware of his surroundings. When he saw the man pacing back and forth near his car, he instinctively felt for the blade in his pocket. But as he came closer, he realized it was just an old man looking like he was lost.

"You okay, Sir?" Dee could still feel the slap on his face when he had not said sir to his grandfather. His mama almost knocked his teeth out for saying "what" to her father when he called his name. It only took that one time to teach him to respect his elders.

"You Dee?" Mr. Lee asked.

Dee was surprised that he knew his name. He nodded his head slowly to confirm that it was him.

"Nice to meet you, Son." Mr. Lee shook his hand firmly. "I need you to help me find my boy."

The two sat in Mr. Lee's car for two hours. He updated him on Alex and told him everything that happened up until that point. Dee sat listening intently. Alex was like his little brother. It made him feel a mixture of sadness and anger that he was with Russ. Dee knew Russ was just using Alex. Russ was a coward. Always had been a coward. Mr. Lee had told him Russ was with Jimmy and that the two of them had tried to break into the group home.

"At first the police made it seem like Alex had something to do with it, but I know that's not true."

"No, Sir." Dee spoke up. "That's not Alex. Alex a good kid. Just got dealt a bad hand."

"I know, Son." Mr. Lee nodded in agreement.

Dee was still sitting in his car when Mr. Lee pulled off. He couldn't let Alex get caught up with Russ and Jimmy. Russ was bad news.

"Where could he be?" Dee asked himself over and over again. He started replaying all the places he thought they could be. He opened his glove compartment and closed it again. It was still there. Dee had left that life, but he also wasn't dumb enough to think that everybody was cool with it. He knew Russ definitely wasn't cool with that. Russ had made a lot of money running for Dee. Truth be told, he still ran for Dee when he was locked up. He held a lot of animosity towards Dee and Dee knew that. It had been over a year since he had seen him, and he had planned to keep it that way, but talking to Mr. Lee showed him that wouldn't be the case for long.

Dee wasn't hiding from his past. It was more like he was running from it. He knew who he had been and took responsibility for everything he had done but it caused too much pain to allow himself to think about it. During the time with Mr. Lee, he had shown him so much compassion when he spoke about understanding Dee's life. Dee was sure that his father loved his family, but he had spent so much time working to provide for them that he didn't really know him the way he wished he had before he died. His grandfather had been his male role model. Mr. Lee had spoken to him about forgiveness and that God doesn't see us as our past mistakes. Even though Dee sometimes went to church with his mother, he couldn't wrap his mind around God ever forgiving him. Here he was, twenty-three years old and with a record thicker than a chapter book. At what point does God stop forgiving? At what point does He say that someone is too far gone?

Dee had promised Mr. Lee he would find out where Alex was; however, Mr. Lee had made Dee promise he would not be the one to get him.

"You have to trust me, Son." Mr. Lee said. "God is going to do this in a way that everyone is as safe as possible. If we do it His way, He will protect us."

It was already after midnight when Dee called his mom to let her know he would be there in a couple of hours. He was going to ride out and ask a couple of people in the area what they knew. When Dee first went straight, everyone avoided him. They thought he had snitched on them in jail, but time made them more comfortable around him. Dee had never turned on anybody when he was locked up, but he also had never gone straight before. Then word got around about JT and his boys understood why Dee had left the streets.

It didn't take long before Dee found out Alex, Russ, and Jimmy were in a hotel outside of Dallas. He knew that hotel all too well. He had done some of everything in that same run-down cheap inn. They had gone there because the cops didn't bother that place too much. It was usually filled with travelers and homeless men and women. Seemed like the world didn't care too much about the ones they didn't think mattered. He parked his car outside of the hotel and leaned his seat back. He looked around the parking lot at the cars and decided that they must be on foot. Russ was notorious for grabbing rental cars here and there or stealing them and ditching them once he was done. That explained why the guy had seen him and Jimmy walking a few blocks away from this same hotel.

His mind wrestled with his heart. He wanted to see Alex with his own eyes, but he didn't know if he would be able to leave him if he did. He also thought about Mr. Lee. He couldn't bring himself to put him in that situation. Dee wasn't sure about the God stuff Mr. Lee was saying. He wasn't sure if God made Mr. Lee bullet or hand proof, but his instinct told him to just trust what Mr. Lee told him.

"When you been with God long enough," Mr. Lee had said. "You know when He is talking. You know what He is saying."

Just then, Dee saw Russ and Jimmy walking out of one of the rooms. He strained to try to see the room number, and when he couldn't, he looked around to at least know which unit it was. A minute later, Alex walked out and stood beside them. Dee smiled. He was taller and bulkier but still the same Alex. Still had that same walk. Still shoving his hands in his pockets and still looking at his feet when he walked. Dee used to joke with him that somebody was going to sneak up on him, and he wasn't even going to see it coming. He thought that for a long time until he saw Alex in action a couple of times. It seemed like Alex just had an on and off switch, and unless something was happening, his switch was off.

Dee headed back home. It was almost two in the morning when he pulled up to his mom's house. The lights were still on, so he knew she had not been able to sleep. This is one reason he tried not to stay gone too long after work. His mom still worried about him, and he knew she would for some time. As soon as he pulled up, he saw the light in her room turn off.

The next morning, as promised, Dee called Mr. Lee. He told him where he had last seen Alex and that he did not want him to go alone.

"I switched shifts so we can go when you ready," Dee told Mr. Lee.

"It's not when I'm ready. It's when God's ready." Mr. Lee responded.

***

**22** “They found Alex,” Jacobson hung up the phone and rushed into the kitchen.

Stacey had been busy meal prepping the past few days. Whenever she was nervous, she either cleaned or cooked. Their freezer had enough food to feed a village during WWIII. She spun around from the stove and pulled off her apron.

Jacobson read her mind.

“We’re not going over there right now, Stace,” he started. “We have to wait.”

“Wait on what?” Stacey raised her voice. “We’ve been waiting for weeks.”

Jacobson smiled at his wife. There was no doubt in his mind that if he or his kids needed to go to battle, they would not go alone. That was one of the reasons he married her. She was fiercely loyal and protective. It was like watching a lioness protect her cubs except Stacey saw everyone she loved as if they were her cubs.

"Babe," Jacobson's voice was calm. "He's safe, and we know where he is. Mr. Lee found Alex's friend, Dee. They are working on a plan. He wants us to pray that God redeems all of them. These are all young boys. We have to remember that. They're lost."

Stacey frowned and crossed her arms. She agreed they were lost but she felt, at that moment, they needed a good old-fashioned, old school whooping. The only thing she thought about was Alex's chubby little legs running to her classroom every morning trying to finish his homework so he wouldn't get in trouble. She thought about how cute he was when he would come to her defense when other students would try to disrespect her even though she didn't need it. She had felt a strong mother's instinct for him. When God brought Alex back into her life, and she learned everything he had gone through, that same need to protect him resurfaced. But she also understood that no one can protect us the way God can. Despite all the evils in the world, He was still a good God and still cared about the outcome of His children.

"Mr. Lee said the guy who Alex was trying to get to has turned his life around," Jacobson waved his hand up in the air.

"What the enemy meant for evil, God used it," he said.

"For good," Stacey finished.

Jacobson updated Stacey on everything Mr. Lee had told him. Neither of them felt good about him going to find Dee on his own, but they also knew Mr. Lee didn't move unless God told him to. God doesn't set us up to cause us harm.

"Sounds like we need to pray for Jimmy and Russ too," Stacey spoke quietly. "God doesn't see people. He sees souls, and all souls matter to Him."

With that, they joined hands and took turns praying for Jimmy and Russ. Stacey prayed for their souls and asked God to block any decisions that would cause them eternal separation or to stop their purpose here on earth.

"Father," Stacey prayed. "So many people on this earth live reckless lives because they don't know their purpose. We pray that you soften their hearts and let them see their lives as ones that are to be lived for you."

When they opened their eyes, they saw Rachel and Joshua holding hands beside them.

"And please," Rachel added. "Jesus please don't let anything happen to Brother Alex and let the bad men who tried to break in the house be good men one day for you."

"Amen, baby" Jacobson reached down to pick her up and give her a hug.

"Let the bad men be good men one day for God," He repeated.

***

**23** By the time they arrived at the group home, Stacey and Jacobson were amazed at what they saw. Mr. Lee had fixed up the remaining two rooms.

Stacey walked around each bedroom in awe of what Mr. Lee had done.

"Did you build this?" Stacey asked while rubbing her hands across the bed frames. She turned and looked at Mr. Lee's beaming face.

"I got bored." He laughed unable to hide his satisfaction and pride.

Jacobson opened the dresser drawer and closed it.

"How? When did you have time?" He asked. Clearly shocked at what he was seeing.

"Well," Mr. Lee grinned. "Been trying to keep busy."

Mr. Lee had built twin sized beds, double dressers, and double desks for each room. The dressers were unique in that he had custom built them into each corner to preserve space in the room. He had even built a small bookshelf for each room.

"Only thing left is to decorate," Mr. Lee pointed at each of the beds. "I figured I'd leave that part to you, Stacey, so you won't go stir crazy when we head out."

"Wait," Stacey turned around. "Who is we?"

"*We* does *not* include you my dear," Mr. Lee spoke in the way that only a father can.

"You and Rose will be here to welcome our boys."

Stacey flinched. She wanted to rebuttal, but she had entirely too much respect for him to argue with him. She looked at Jacobson who shrugged his shoulders.

"God is the commander, and Mr. Lee is the captain," Jacobson smiled. "I'm just a soldier ready to do as I'm told."

Stacey rolled her eyes at Jacobson and walked towards the door.

"Wait a second," she stopped mid step. "Did you say our boys?"

Mr. Lee closed his eyes and nodded his head slowly back and forth.

"God's plan," he answered. "All God's plan."

***

It was early evening when Dee met up with Mr. Lee at his request. Since it was Saturday, he was free. He wasn't sure what the plan was, but he made sure he was ready for however it needed to go. He hoped for the best but, if he were honest, he never really allowed himself to believe that his life would be any different than the ones he had seen. The part of him that wanted life to be different was always in conflict with the part that lived in reality. Today was one of those days he decided could very well end in a way that didn't put him at an advantage. He wasn't going to let Russ hurt Alex or Mr. Lee. He knew that for sure. In a hand-to-hand fight, Alex would win, but Russ was not a hand-to-hand type of guy. He stopped fighting fair when his losses outnumbered his wins.

All he knew was that Mr. Lee asked him to meet him two blocks from the hotel and instructed him to stay in the car. He promised he would but knew in his heart that promise may have to be broken.

A few minutes later, Mr. Lee pulled up in his vehicle. There was another car behind him. Mr. Lee stepped out of his car and motioned for the others. He introduced Jacobson to Dee and went over the plan.

"With all due respect Mr. Lee, I can't let you go in alone," Dee interrupted. Mr. Lee had informed Jacobson and Dee to remain in their vehicles, and he would go in and get Alex. "I don't know about God and all that, but I do know streets and the streets don't have no fear or respect for God."

Mr. Lee was quiet and stared off in the direction of the hotel.

Without a word, he held up his shirt. It was covered in scars.

"I know about the streets, *and* I know about God." He pulled his shirt down and pointed them to their cars.

Jacobson and Dee stood momentarily frozen. Mr. Lee looked like he had been sliced up and down, then put back together again.

With that single motion, he turned around and walked away.

"How do you even know they're there?" Dee yelled out.

"I know," Mr. Lee answered and kept walking down the street.

Dee looked at Jacobson almost in panic. "Listen. Russ is dangerous. He won't kill that old man, but he'll get Jimmy to do it 'cause Jimmy slow as syrup."

Jacobson paced back and forth. This definitely wasn't what he had in mind either. Part of him wanted to follow Mr. Lee while the other part wanted to call the police.

"Yeah," Jacobson tried to hide his nervousness while praying in his head. "Let's just wait and see what happens.

"I'm cool with waiting," Dee said. "But I'm gonna wait closer to the hotel." With that, he grabbed a bag from his trunk and started walking in the direction of the hotel.

Instinctively, Jacobson followed.

***

Mr. Lee walked the two blocks to get to the hotel. He prayed the entire way. He was calm and ready. He knew what God had showed him, and he trusted that this would work out for the good of them all.

He was a few feet from the hotel when he heard someone run up behind him. Before he could turn around, he felt cold metal pressed up against the back of his head.

"I knew you were gonna try something old man," The voice behind him said. "I saw you casing the place. Who you lookin' for?"

Mr. Lee took a deep breath.

"I'm looking for my boy. Just trying to get him back home," he answered without turning around.

"Well, he ain't here," The voice said. "Nobody out here that belong to nobody else. Ain't no families out here."

Mr. Lee slowly put his hands out to show he wasn't a threat, but right when he did that, he looked up and saw Alex, Russ, and Jimmy heading in his direction. Fear tried to grip him because he was sure Alex would react if he saw someone holding a gun to his head.

"You're right, young man." Mr. Lee kept his voice calm. "I'll just turn around and go back to my car."

"Not before you hand me whatever that is sticking out your pocket," He took the gun and patted Mr. Lee's left pocket.

Mr. Lee reached down carefully and pulled out his wallet. He held it to the side and the man snatched it.

It was then he realized Alex, Jimmy, and Russ were getting closer. So close that Russ pointed him and the guy out.

"I think ole dude robbing that ole man," Russ stopped. Jimmy and Alex looked in his direction.

"That's messed up," Jimmy said.

"Let's go," Russ redirected them to head in the opposite direction, but Alex stayed in the same spot staring. Mr. Lee could tell by his body language he realized it was him. He started walking toward them.

"Look," Mr. Lee tried to act quickly. "I don't want no problems young man. Just take the wallet and go."

The man grabbed the wallet, but then stopped when he saw Alex walking toward him. Judging by how fast the guy was walking and the two guys trying to catch up with him, he knew it was about to be trouble. He welcomed trouble.

"Aye, man," Jimmy asked Alex. "Let that go. That ain't our problem.

"I know him," Alex said under his breath.

"Ah, shhh," Russ patted Jimmy. "If it wasn't for the fact that my grandpops raised me, I'd be trippin. Let's go."

With Jimmy, Alex, and Russ heading towards Mr. Lee, the guy finally was able to take his attention off him.

He pushed Mr. Lee away from him and waved his gun in the direction of the boys.

Russ hesitated as Jimmy put his hand in his waist showing that he was ready. Alex kept walking toward Mr. Lee.

"Hey man," Alex spoke fearlessly. "He good. He with us. He don't want no problems with you."

"Come on, Mr. Lee." By then, Alex was a few feet from him with Russ and Jimmy behind him.

The man looked at all four of them and laughed.

"Nah, young blood," he said. "He must want problems if he out here looking for them."

"Young man," Mr. Lee felt strength well up in him when he saw Alex. He felt an overwhelming calm.

"I don't want no problems. I only came to get what belongs to my Father."

For the first time since this happened, he turned around to face the voice behind him. The young man looked like he was in his early twenties, and even though he held firm to the weapon in his hand, Mr. Lee knew he didn't really want to use it.

But from behind him, he could see Dee and Jacobson coming up. He instinctively yelled out to them to stop.

The young man looked behind him, realizing he was surrounded. He pointed the gun at Mr. Lee and said, "What kinda business you runnin' out here, Ole Man?"

Mr. Lee could hear the fear in his voice and knew this situation was dangerous for all of them.

Russ elbowed Jimmy who pulled his gun from his waist. Dee instinctively pulled one from his backpack.

Time slowed down, and Mr. Lee could feel a burning sensation in his stomach. He opened his mouth and yelled out:

"In the name of Jesus, no lives with be lost on this day. In the name of Jesus, every young man under the sound of my voice will live and not die and declare the works of the Lord."

Everyone around him stopped. Mr. Lee held onto the authority he knew he had been given by his Heavenly Father.

"I take authority over premature death, and I command every spirit of murder and sabotage to release all of you in the name of Jesus."

All the young men froze. They didn't know what to do. It was as if someone had grabbed them and held them to their spots.

"There will be no death on this day. There will be no lives lost on this day. You have no authority over them anymore. The Lord God rebuke you," Mr. Lee was pointing in every direction no longer speaking to the young men.

"You have wasted too much of their lives, and you did not give them life. Their lives belong to our Father. Their future belongs to our Father. You will release them in the name of Jesus. They will be servants of the Most High God."

Mr. Lee was sweating and pacing back and forth. The man who had held the gun was frozen in fear. He felt the gun slide from his hands and stood as if he was being held in place by something bigger than him. Jacobson nodded for Dee to put his gun away, but Dee couldn't move. Jacobson took the gun from his hand and put it on the ground.

"I have come in the power of the Most High God to reclaim what you have attempted to steal." Mr. Lee yelled at the top of his voice.

Alex felt the same pride well up in him he felt when he would hear Mr. Lee praying for him in the middle of the night.

"Put that up, Jimmy." Alex told him. Jimmy had been standing there frozen with his gun in his hand but didn't move. Alex looked over and saw tears falling from his eyes. He couldn't stop them from rolling down his face. He looked at Russ, normally the instigator, and saw that he had turned his back. He was wiping his face, so Alex knew he too was crying.

Mr. Lee called out to the angels of God to circle around all of them and to follow them wherever they went. He called on the Holy Spirit to show the young men that Jesus did not give his life for them to lose their own.

"I call on every broken part of you to be covered and healed and every generational curse to be cancelled in the name of Jesus."

Mr. Lee fell to his knees, and instinctively, Alex and Jacobson ran toward him. But Mr. Lee lifted his arms in surrender and cried out:

"Thank you, Jesus. They're coming home."

**23** "Man, you look like a straight up cornball with that bow tie on," Russ walked over to Alex and playfully grabbed him.

"They gonna have you looking the same way at your graduation," Alex laughed.

"That's if he graduates," Jimmy laughed. "Mrs. Johnson gave him one last extension for this project. I think this fool think she jokin'." Russ had been enrolled in a dual trade and high school equivalency program while Jimmy had been attending a trade program through the boy's home.

Mr. Lee walked out of their shared living area.

"There's no if," he laughed. "One down and two more to go."

"Yessir," Russ smiled. "Yessir."

Just then Jacobson and Stacey walked into the house with the kids, followed by Dee.

Stacey hugged all of them.

"Look at my guys!" She couldn't contain herself while looking at the three young men who God had allowed her to witness turn their lives around. In one short year, God had done miracle after miracle. The day Mr. Lee returned with all of them, including the young man, Robert, who had held him at gunpoint was a day she will never forget. He had taken them under his wings and showed them mercy that leads to redemption. It was a true miracle. Mr. Lee knew he would come home with Russ, Jimmy, and Alex. He did not know that God would use him to rescue Robert and Dee as well. God used Mr. Lee to bond all of them to Him and each other. They looked out for each other, and even though Robert did not live with them or attend any of their programs, he came over weekly for Bible study and dinner. He too had turned his life around, and Dee had gotten him a job at the same warehouse he worked in.

***

"I never would have thought it would end the way it ended," Stacey looked at Mr. Lee fighting back tears of gratitude.

"God does more than we ever ask or think," Mr. Lee nodded his head slowly as he spoke. "This is His doing, and it is marvelous in his eyes."

I pray that the eyes of your heart may be enlightened in order that you may know the hope to which he has called you, the riches of his glorious inheritance in his holy people.

Ephesians 1: 18

I dedicate this book to all the young people who have lost their way. I pray that God shows you how absolutely beautifully and wonderfully you are made. Don't you dare give up before you see what you were created to be!

John 3: 16

For God so loved the world that he gave his one and only Son, that whoever believes in him shall not perish but have eternal life.